"Ryder? Have you ever had great sex?"

His hands froze for a second, then resumed massaging. "Yeah. A very long time ago. At least, I remember it as being great."

"I never have," Marti continued. "I thought it was one big disappointment and couldn't understand why it was such a huge deal."

Again his hands froze. Then he whispered, "Oh, lady, you just handed me a grenade."

She opened her eyes to half-mast. "Grenade? What do you mean?"

"I've been wanting you since I laid eyes on you. Now you've all but asked me. Tell me you don't mean it."

"Why?"

"You know all the reasons. You're pregnant. I'll be leaving eventually to go see Ben. I'm an emotional train wreck....Why in God's name would you want to get mixed up with me even temporarily?"

She barely hesitated. "Because I want to know."

Dear Reader,

In life things can happen that leave us emotionally devastated. Some things also leave us with so much self-doubt we have trouble dealing with them, and little in the way of logic or argument can make us feel any better.

Marti is pregnant and widowed. A tornado has devastated her home. Ryder comes into her life as a man she rescued from the storm, and he stays to help her put things to rights again. Ryder carries a heavy burden of guilt over the loss of his wife, and helping Marti makes him feel useful again. And Marti discovers that she is deserving of the big and little things Ryder wants to do for her.

Ryder is by nature a hands-on fixer, a guy with a background in construction that he is only too willing to put to work again for Marti. The work helps him heal, Marti helps him heal and he helps her find her self-worth.

In the process of rebuilding Marti's home, they rebuild themselves and each other, then face a threat as deadly as any tornado, one that brings them to the realization that they are loved.

The heart triumphs. It often does. Enjoy!

Rachel Lee

RACHEL LEE

The Widow's Protector

ROMANTIC

SUSPENSE

Recycling programs
for this product may
not exist in your area.

ISBN-13: 978-0-373-27777-3

THE WIDOW'S PROTECTOR

www.Harlequin.com

Printed in U.S.A.

Books by Rachel Lee

RACHEL LEE

was hooked on writing by the age of twelve, and practiced her craft as she moved from place to place all over the United States. *This New York Times* bestselling author now resides in Florida and has the joy of writing full-time.

To my readers, who bring so much joy into my life.

Prologue

Ben Hansen hung up the phone, and he was furious. He'd been furious ever since Brandy had killed herself, and he knew who was responsible. Of course he knew who was responsible. Brandy hadn't had a single problem until she'd married that dolt Ryder Kelstrom.

That was when the sickness started, and Ben didn't need a map to tell him who had made Brandy so depressed. But damn it, he wished Ryder would just get his butt out here.

He'd looked for an opportunity to pay the guy back at the funeral in New York and hadn't been able to get Ryder alone for even ten seconds. Even if he had, he'd have left too much evidence behind.

No, he reminded himself. He needed to get Ryder away from anyone who would even know he was there. Then he'd deal with him.

He'd pushed Ryder to come out to Fresno by himself, but instead of hopping a plane, the guy had decided to take the bus and hike. Weeks. Weeks! And Ben had already been waiting eight months for his opportunity.

At first he'd thought Ryder's trip would make it easier. The guy was in the middle of nowhere, for God's sake, where no one knew him. If something happened to him, they'd never trace it back here to Fresno.

But the trip was taking too long, and Ryder never said exactly where he was.

Drumming his fingers on the table, Ben counseled himself to patience. At some point he'd figure out where Ryder was planning to travel. At some point he'd pin the guy down.

And then he was going to leave Ryder to bleed to death just the way Brandy had.

Chapter 1

Ryder Kelstrom strolled along one of Wyoming's dusty roads in no particular hurry. He'd chosen the slowest way possible of getting from the East Coast to the West because he had a lot of emotional baggage he wanted to deal with before he met his brother-in-law in Fresno. So here he was, hiking along some desolate county road in a place he'd never heard of, with only a map to guide him to the next town and the next bus station.

Fine by him. He was still sorting through a lot, trying to make sense out of the insanity. He felt events settling inside him, but understanding was still beyond reach. Maybe it always would be.

The sky was turning an ugly black-green, and the clouds hung low and heavy. Getting wet didn't worry him, though. He'd managed to live most of his life outdoors, working construction and eventually owning his own building business. He wasn't one to fear the elements except as a possible delay on a contractual deadline. Right now he didn't have any deadlines at all.

Wind pushed at him suddenly, at first chilly enough that he buttoned up his denim jacket. After another half-mile, though, it suddenly turned warmer.

That was odd. He looked up again and could have sworn some of those inky clouds would have scraped treetops if there had been any trees in sight. These wide-open spaces had become familiar to him in his travels, but it still astonished him sometimes to realize he could look horizon to horizon and not see any sign of habitation. He was used to the denser population of the East, and the seemingly empty spaces he'd found since hitting the Midwest delighted him. It was almost possible to feel as if he were alone on the planet.

Certainly he felt utterly alone these days.

The wind buffeted him again, still warm, nearly knocking him off his feet. He staggered a bit then kept on walking. He was definitely going to get wet. A crackle of lightning in one of the clouds concerned him, though. He seemed to be the tallest thing around for miles.

He heard an engine roaring up from behind him, but he didn't bother to stick out a thumb. It was okay to get wet, and he really wasn't in a mood to converse with a stranger. And these days thumbing a ride didn't get you very far very fast. Most people knew better than to pick up hitchhikers and, as he'd already learned from a cop, hitchhiking was now illegal in many places.

But the engine roared up beside him, and he glanced over to see a woman in a battered pickup pacing him. What the hell?

She turned her head and shouted out to him. "Get in. There's a tornado coming and I have a shelter."

He shook his head. "I'll be fine, ma'am. I may get wet, but what's the likelihood a tornado will find me? Slim, don't you think?"

"You don't understand," she shouted as the wind picked up. "This tornado is a mile wide!"

That drew him up short. A mile wide? He'd never seen a tornado in his life outside of news programs, but even so he could appreciate the size of that danger. He'd have to be really foolish to stay out here.

He turned and she braked the truck to let him climb in. He pulled the heavy backpack off his shoulders, tossing it on the floorboard. When he slid into the passenger seat, he couldn't help but notice that she was pretty, with blond ringlets around her face and nicely delineated features. The kind that would be photogenic for sure.

Nor could he escape noticing that she was pregnant. Very pregnant. No judge of such things, he could only guess that she was in her last trimester.

Before he could register more, she hammered the accelerator and dirt and gravel spun out behind them in the seconds before they gained traction. Then they were speeding down the rutted road, bouncing like balls inside the cab.

"It's coming this way," she said, her voice tight. "Straight at us. My place is only a couple of minutes from here." A huge tumbleweed raced across the road in front of them, but she didn't even slow down.

"Maybe it will blow out," he suggested, trying to offer hope.

"Not likely when it's this big."

What did he know? Just what he'd picked up from

casual viewing of the news and weather broadcasts. A mile wide? Instinctively he felt she was right: it wasn't going to die very soon, not with that much power in it.

She rounded a bend in the road and he could have almost sworn two of the wheels lifted from the ground. As they swung around, he got a different view of the sky. Now those black clouds seemed to have reached the earth. Was that the tornado?

Drops of rain splattered the dusty windshield. She ignored it. Ahead he could finally see a small farmhouse sheltered by a circle of trees. A few hundred yards away stood an ancient-looking barn. The buildings seemed to be in a slight dip, which had concealed them from him earlier. She headed straight for the buildings as if she wanted to win the Indy 500.

At the last minute she veered, throwing him against the truck's door. This woman was giving no ground to anything in her determination to reach safety. Her fear reached him and made him even more concerned about the weather's threat.

She braked hard and switched off the ignition. "Come on!"

He jumped out, slamming the truck's door, although he wasn't sure it would do a damn bit of good as it seemed the sky had come to earth, inky green, and was racing toward them.

She ran. He worried that she might stumble but she didn't. Then out of tall grasses he spied a metal door in the ground. She bent to open it, but he brushed her hand aside and did the heavy work himself.

It was a heavy steel door. "Get in," he yelled at her as the wind began to howl and tried to pull the door from his grip. She hurried down some cement stairs, vanishing into the ground. Waiting only a second, he followed, battling to drag the door shut behind him.

The day outside had grown as dark as night, but still he glimpsed the bolts that would hold the door closed. There was a moment of struggle, then he banged it shut. Feeling around, he found the heavy bolts and drove them home.

Even with the door shut, he could hear the banshee's wail of the wind outside. He waited.

Then a flashlight beam punctured the darkness, lighting the stairs.

"Come down," she said, her voice shaking, "in case the door goes."

He obeyed and found himself in a tight shelter. It might have held six or eight people at most, but it had a few comforts: a couple of benches, flashlights, a battery-operated radio. It was enough to survive the onslaught.

By the glow of the flashlight, he watched her twist her hands nervously as she listened to the wind howl. He tried to think of something reassuring to say, but he couldn't imagine what. There was a tornado coming and they could do nothing but ride it out.

"My house," she said, fear edging her voice.

"Worry about that if you have to," he said as gently as he could. "We don't know. It might miss you entirely."

"I hope so."

"What about your husband? He's not home I gather."

"He's dead," she said baldly.

He sure as hell didn't know how to respond to that. A woman so far along in pregnancy, and she had no husband to help her? That was pretty bad all by itself, especially out here in what seemed to him, at least, to be the middle of nowhere. "Anybody else?"

"I haven't lived here that long. I don't really know anybody but my doctor."

He was sure this line of conversation wasn't making her feel any better. When she reached over and switched on the battery-operated radio, he was glad of it.

Static hissed loudly, and a mechanical voice advised there was a tornado warning for all of Conard County. It advised taking shelter immediately because there was a large funnel moving northeast from the state highway. Several other funnels had been spotted.

"That's not good," she said, her voice thin. He watched her gaze trail to the storm door that protected them, and just at that moment something banged it hard. They both jumped a little.

The mechanical warning kept repeating in the background, fading out completely to static from time to time. How long could this go on? Ryder wondered. Only a few minutes, surely. But how would they know whether the storm was still approaching and when it had passed? Maybe they'd get an all-clear.

She looked ghastly in the flashlight's beam, and her face seemed to grow more pinched with every second.

"I guess I should introduce myself," he said, hoping to distract her. "I'm Ryder Kelstrom."

Her frightened gaze left the door and returned to him. "Marti Chastain."

"When's the baby coming?"

"About two months."

"That's soon."

"It feels like forever sometimes."

But he noted the protective way she folded her arms over her belly, cradling her unborn child.

"Boy or girl?" he asked.

"Girl. I'm going to call her Linda Marie."

"That's pretty." Maybe talking about the baby was the ticket, he decided, not that he had a whole lot of experience with pregnant women. His own wife had never wanted to conceive, a good thing given how it had all turned out. It was hard enough to explain her suicide to himself without having to explain it to a child.

"Have you got everything ready?"

Before she could answer, however, something else slammed the steel door, nearly deafening them, and then a steady hammering began. Hail maybe. It was loud enough to drown out the radio, which might actually be a mercy.

"I'm from back East," he remarked, raising his voice to be heard, trying more distraction. "I'm not used to this."

"I'm not used to this, either," she called back. "I've only been here a few months. I never expected this."

"Nobody does," he agreed. "I bet even the people who live in Tornado Alley don't expect it'll hit them."

"Probably not."

But she was looking at the door again, as if she feared it might give way under the assault. He kind of wondered himself, although he'd felt its heft and weight and judged it to be sturdy. But he had no idea how it might react to a truly powerful tornado. Photos of heaped debris didn't tell him much about the tensile strength of a door like that, just a lot about the tensile strength of the wood used in construction.

"Do you work?" he asked as the elements beat on the door like an insane drummer.

"What?" Her face turned back to him. "Oh. No. I didn't need to, at least not until after the baby—" She broke off sharply as the storm's giant fist pounded the door again.

Who would have thought, Ryder wondered, that you might need ear protection in a storm shelter?

Then, so suddenly as to be startling, the world fell absolutely silent.

After a few seconds, she whispered in the silence. "It can't be over yet. That was a big storm."

He agreed. "The tornado might have passed, but the weather still has to be threatening. I guess we should wait for an all-clear from the radio."

"I guess." She wrapped her arms more tightly around her belly, protectively. "The house. It's all I really have."

"Do you have insurance?"

She shook her head. "We couldn't afford it. My husband inherited it, and when he lost his job we moved out here. We figured we could make it on land leases until one of us found work."

"Then you lost him. So no income at all?"

"Just from the leases. There's a lot of land. We've leased it to grow hay, and some as grazing land. It's not a lot, but it was enough for the basics."

She glanced at the door again as the drumming resumed.

"Everything may be okay," he said pointlessly. Although it was easy to tell someone not to worry about things they didn't know, and they certainly didn't know if anything had happened to her house, worry seemed to be a natural human state.

He hated sitting here like this, unable to do anything but wait, and if he hated it, so must she. She had a lot more at stake. But if he'd learned anything at all from his marriage to Brandy, it was that sometimes no amount of effort could solve a problem.

Of course, he still wasn't sure which lessons to take from that. It didn't seem to have improved his patience any. But Brandy had tested his patience for years. He'd learned to roll with the punches and deal with each day as it came. Maybe that was the maximum patience a man could learn.

The radio crackled and a voice came back, telling them the tornado warning had been lifted for Conard County.

Then Marti reached out to switch the dial, and a staticky news station came on. The sheriff reported that damage to Conard City appeared to be minimal, but they were still awaiting reports from outlying areas. Power and telephones were out, and some cell towers seemed to be down. The station pleaded for folks to check on their neighbors and find a way to report emergencies to the sheriff's department.

Marti looked at the closed storm door again, and Ryder could read the anxiety in every line of her. She needed to look but was afraid to.

Finally, despite the drumbeat of what he assumed to be rain, Ryder realized that nothing heavy was battering them any longer, and the wind had stopped wailing. Time to check.

He climbed the stairs, unlocked the bolts and threw the door back.

"Oh my God," he heard Marti say on a breath right behind him.

If it hadn't passed right overhead, the tornado had certainly come close. He saw a cluster of debris around the shelter opening, and beyond it he could see her house.

Part of the roof was gone and some of the trees had come down, although not on the house, the only mercy he could see. The tree trunks looked like splintered matchwood, giving him some idea of the power of the storm that had just passed them.

He shoved debris aside, making a clear path for the woman behind him. He didn't want her tripping on anything.

Then he climbed out and turned to offer her a hand. Steady rain fell, although not heavily, and the sky had lightened to a deep gray. The inky green was gone.

But so was part of her life.

Marti stood there staring at her house, the one thing she had counted on to get her through, taking in the corner of the roof that had been stripped of its covering, leaving rafters bare. *The rain would get in,* she thought numbly. *It would ruin everything.*

The downed trees didn't shock her as much, though it troubled her to see them. They had provided protection in the winter from the wind and then shade as spring had deepened. Now they were just kindling.

Then, feeling as if every muscle in her body had turned to lead, she pivoted to look out over the fields that had been planted with hay.

"Oh my God," she said again, clapping one hand to her mouth. The hay had been mown right down to the bare earth as if by a giant scythe, along a line so clearly marked she could have believed a surveyor had laid it. It told her how close that tornado had come, missing her buildings by a couple of hundred feet. And the slash was so wide.

"My God," she said helplessly. There went her income. Nobody was going to be able to pay up on those leases if they lost their crop.

Her knees started to weaken, and she was grateful when Ryder gripped her elbow, steadying her.

"It's gone," she whispered hollowly. "It's all gone." What was she supposed to do now?

"Do you have any decent tarps?" Ryder asked her.

Slowly her gaze tracked to him. Any other time she would have thought him a fine-looking man, with his chiseled, slightly weathered face, his lean, hard build. Those gray eyes of his were filled with compassion, and the compassion almost made her weep. How long had it been since anyone had given a damn about her?

Not that it mattered. He was a stranger she had picked up along the roadside only because she couldn't leave another human being out in this storm. He'd probably resume his trek in a matter of minutes.

"Tarps?" she repeated blankly.

"I need to cover that hole in your roof before the rain does too much damage."

"You don't have to...." She had trouble grasping that he was offering to help in some way. The idea didn't want to penetrate the haze of total despair.

"I have to," he said. "It's the least I can do. Looks like you saved my life. Tarps?" he repeated.

"In the barn," she said woodenly. "I think there are some there."

"Okay." His steadying grip on her elbow tightened a bit. "I want you to stay in the truck out of the rain. Come on."

She was in no condition to argue. What would she argue about anyway? There was nothing she could do herself, not in her condition.

So she let him guide her back to the truck, let him help her climb back in.

"Just stay," he said, his gray eyes stern. "I can at least keep the rain out if I can find enough tarps."

"Thank you." It was a paltry expression of gratitude, but she was having trouble feeling grateful about anything right now. The baby inside her kicked, and she laid her hand over the spot. The baby. Whatever she did about this, the baby had to be her first concern. Her only concern. If that meant moving on…

She couldn't even consider it then. She stared at the house, stared at the hole in her roof, then watched Ryder trek to the barn through the rain. Why couldn't it have been the barn roof?

Sometimes she just wanted to yell at the heavens. But right now she didn't even have energy for that. The devastation she saw everywhere she looked… Well, right now she didn't even feel grateful for having survived.

Then the baby kicked again, reminding her why she had to carry on. The baby, she murmured to herself, over and over. Whatever came next, she had to do it for Linda Marie.

The tears came then, silent large drops that rolled down her face like rain.

Ryder took a flashlight to the barn with him, well aware that what he was about to do was dangerous. It was still raining, and he could hear rumbles of thunder. There was some small hail on the ground, too, which could make planting a ladder dangerous, and there might be more. What did he know about storms like this? He was no meteorologist.

But he just couldn't bring himself to walk away from this woman's problem without at least protecting her house from more damage. Rain getting in would do far more to cause her problems than the tornado had.

So he started hunting the unfamiliar space. The flashlight at least picked up on an aluminum ladder quickly, one that looked of recent vintage and would get him up the twenty feet he needed to climb to the roof.

Hammer and nails were next, easily found in the tack room at the back. Some of the nails looked a bit rusty with age, but they weren't bad. Enough to do a temporary job. The tarps gave him more trouble, although he couldn't imagine a place like this, if it had ever been worked, would lack them. A lot of things you might want to leave outdoors needed to be protected from rain and the inevitable rust or mold.

It seemed to take forever, but at last he found a stack of them, musty and heavy. They weren't the lighter-weight new ones, but as he checked them, he thought they would do. Canvas, and full of clay to judge by the weight. If they leaked anywhere, that's what they made buckets for.

With some rope, he bound them together in stacks he felt he could carry on his back up a ladder. An old tool belt came in handy for carrying hammer and nails.

When he stepped back outside, the day had darkened again. The smell of the earth, freshly churned by the passing tornado, filled his nostrils. But at least it had stopped raining for the moment.

He set up the ladder against a part of the roof that hadn't been damaged, settling it carefully in the wet ground, then began lugging up the stuff he would need. A streak of lightning rent the sky to the west, followed by a low rumble of thunder.

He needed his head examined. At any work site he had supervised, he'd have stopped all exterior work while something like this was going on. But in this case, he felt he had no choice. Who knew how much rain would fall and how much damage Marti's house would suffer? It was easy to deal with broken wood compared to water damage.

And given the news report, he doubted anyone would come by here soon to help. Hell, probably a lot of her neighbors were trying to do exactly the same thing right now.

Damn tornado.

Up on the roof at last with everything he needed, he studied the problem, deciding how best to nail the tarps into place. At least the storm hadn't removed the underlying roof trusses when it had torn away shingles, tar paper and plywood decking. The gable pieces were still firm and steady to his touch, and he was able to stand on joists some of the time as he worked his way across the opening.

Right then he'd have given just about anything for a nail gun or a heavy-duty staple gun. Instead he had to hammer each nail individually as he attached the tarps.

Rain swept across him from time to time, and occasionally the wind snatched at the tarps, but he lost himself in the comfort of working with his hands. He had always loved working this way, much more so than he had enjoyed running his own business.

Manual labor made him feel good, and before long he was feeling better than he had in months. That ought to tell him something, he thought bitterly. Hard work was good for the heart, body and soul.

Maybe that was what he needed more than anything. More than trying to sort things out in his head, things that didn't sort at all because they knew no logic. Maybe he just needed to work, and work hard, until all the confusion settled and he found the missing pieces of himself that Brandy had taken with her.

He didn't even realize that he had grown soaked to the skin. He didn't notice when the wind took on a bit of a chill.

Hammering nails was good. If nothing else in life could at the moment, the feel of a hammer in his hands and the force he exerted with every downward swing satisfied him.

Sort of like a primal scream, he thought wryly, and reached for another nail. He was exorcising a whole lot of unhappiness and anger and confusion with every blow of that hammer.

Lightning jagged across the sky, followed so closely by a clap of thunder that it reminded him how foolhardy he was being. He wouldn't have let any man who worked for him do this. But he felt he had no choice. The more rain, the higher the likelihood that Marti Chastain's house would suffer severe damage. He couldn't leave anyone like that, least of all a pregnant widow.

She was a pretty woman, he thought as he struggled against the wind to hammer down the last tarp. Pretty with her short blond curls, and pretty in her pregnancy. Funny, he'd never before noticed that a woman so far along could be sexy. But maybe that was because he hadn't been looking. Every bit of him had been utterly focused on Brandy for a long time now.

Okay, so Marti Chastain was a sexy-looking woman, but he felt guilty for even noticing, given her pregnancy and the current state of her life. That woman sure had a whole heap of troubles.

At last he got the final tarp nailed into place, just in time for another wave of heavy rain to sweep through. Sitting on the roof nearby, he watched the water roll off the tarps with satisfaction. Now he'd just need to check inside the attic and see if there were any leaks.

When the rain lightened a bit, he tested the ladder. It still felt stable, so he climbed down cautiously. The rungs were wet but gripped his hiking boots well enough, and the ladder didn't tip at all until he had only a few more steps to take.

When he reached the ground, he carried the ladder and tools back to the barn. There he found an old rag and wiped as best he could at the hammer and nails. The ladder could dry on its own.

The barn roof leaked in a couple of places, he noticed, and he almost sighed. At least the drips weren't falling on anything important, but the idea of another leaking roof bothered the builder in him. Things like that needed fixing to protect a structure, and he had a feeling Marti couldn't afford it.

Great.

As he exited the barn, he saw Marti had left the truck and was now standing on her front porch. He trotted over to her, taking in her dejected posture and the way her blue eyes seemed too large for her face.

"Everything okay?" he asked.

"I was going to ask you that. Thank you for what you did."

"It was nothing." He stepped up on the porch beside

her, out of the rain. "I'd like to check the attic, though. If there are any leaks, we need to put buckets or some- thing under them to catch the water so your ceilings don't collapse."

She nodded, looking out over the destruction again before shaking herself. "Let me make you something to eat," she said. "And you should stay the night. I'm not sure I can get you to town when the road is so soggy. Well, I probably could, but then the question would be whether I could get home. Ruts get deep fast when it's this wet. Plus," she added almost as an afterthought, as if the enormity hadn't really hit her, "some of the roads could be blocked by debris."

He couldn't argue with that.

"You're all wet," she remarked. "You must be freez- ing. Do you have a change?"

"My backpack's in the truck."

"Well, go get it. I'll start a meal."

He jogged over to the truck, which she had brought closer to the house, and wondered what he was doing. Part of him, most of him, just wanted to resume his trav- els even in this inclement weather. He wouldn't melt, and the solitude had been quieting his emotional pangs.

But he also realized that Marti was just being neigh- borly, trying to thank him for putting those tarps on her roof, and she'd probably feel bad if he just marched off into the quieting storm without accepting any mark of her gratitude, whether it was a meal and a bed or a ride to town.

He could identify with that, being pretty much built the same himself, but he looked down the road with a moment of longing as he retrieved his backpack.

Not now, he thought, slinging the heavy pack over

his shoulder. At the very least, he needed to make sure her house was snug and safe. He wouldn't rest easy unless he did.

He needed to check more than the roof. The wind had to have struck awfully hard to tear away that portion, and there might be hidden damage.

Then he started thinking about her leaking barn. Her advanced state of pregnancy. Her lack of friends or family in these parts.

Aw hell, he thought as he tromped back to the house. He couldn't leave with a clear conscience. Not yet. Maybe not for a week or so.

Ben was just going to have to wait a little longer.

Chapter 2

Marti sent Ryder up to change in the guest room, telling him to feel free to use the hall shower, and anything that was in there, if he wanted. It wasn't much of a room. The iron bedstead looked as if it had been there since the house had been built back around 1902, but the mattress had been replaced at some point and was in great condition. The bedding was fresh, too—since she'd had a burst of energy just a week ago and washed all the linens. A battered but large old chest of drawers completed the furnishings. Minimalist but adequate.

She pulled a thawed chicken out of the fridge. She had been planning to roast it tonight anyway and use the leftovers for meals during the week. Ryder looked like he might have a big appetite, but if the chicken disappeared at one sitting, it wasn't as if she'd be left hungry. She had other things in her freezer to cook if she needed them.

But after the way he had climbed up on her roof, braving the elements, to protect her house from further damage, there was no way she was going to let him just leave without a decent meal and a night's sleep.

She'd been scared watching him up there. Sometimes the lightning had seemed so close, and then those bands of rain had blown through with strong winds and she had seen him struggle with the tarps. Fear that he might get struck by lightning or take a fall had never been far from her mind.

What would she have done if he had gotten hurt? Her phone was out, and she couldn't have moved him by herself, certainly not in her present condition.

His willingness to risk his neck to save her from additional damage was startling. She wasn't used to men like that. Jeff, her late husband, probably would have shrugged, popped the top off another beer and told her he'd get to it when the storm passed. If he got to it at all.

Although, seriously, she didn't see how he could have avoided it. This house and the land was all that had stood between them and starvation.

It wasn't like they could sell it. Jeff had tried that when he first lost his job, but nobody was buying run-down farms in the middle of nowhere. At least not at a price Jeff considered fair, assuming he ever had an offer. He'd said not, but as she had learned, Jeff hadn't always told the truth.

She sighed, rubbing the chicken with olive oil and seasonings after rinsing it. Good thing she had a propane stove, because the power seemed to be out, too.

She had better get out a couple of oil lamps before the day got any darker.

They were in the pantry, and while she was in there getting them, she found a package of wild rice a friend had given her before they had moved out here, and she decided that now was as good a time as any to make it. Jeff hadn't liked it, and she'd never felt right about making it just for herself.

So Ryder provided an excuse to go all-out on a meal for the first time in a long while. Cooking for one and eating all by herself rarely inspired her to get fancy.

A loud crack of thunder startled her and the baby kicked in response. "It's all right," she murmured, rubbing her belly gently. How she longed for the day she'd actually be able to hold her daughter in her arms.

She lit the two lamps, heard the shower running upstairs and smiled at how suddenly and unexpectedly this place felt homey. While the elements raged outside, she was cozy in her house, saved by a total stranger, and she was going to have company for dinner.

She decided that for tonight she wasn't going to worry about how she would manage to fix her roof. Wasn't going to worry about anything.

As she had learned all too well, life brought contentment only rarely.

The power was out, the shower had been lukewarm at best, but Ryder felt considerably refreshed as he headed back downstairs in a fresh flannel shirt and dry jeans. His walking boots were sodden, so he'd switched to a pair of joggers, which made his feet feel suddenly light.

He found Marti in the kitchen. The first sizzling of a

roasting chicken filled the air with its aromas, and she was perking a pot of coffee on the stove top.

"Thanks for the shower," he said. "I needed it."

She turned from the stove. "Thanks for covering my roof. It needed it." Then she smiled. The expression was unexpected, warm and genuine. In fact, it almost stole his breath. He felt a little icicle in his heart crack.

"Um…" He had to hunt for words as he drank in that smile. "I need to check your attic for leaks. How do I get there?"

"There's a drop-down ladder in the hall at the end away from the guest room." She paused to rummage in a drawer, then handed him a big flashlight. "You'll need this. You probably noticed the electricity is out."

"I did. I'm afraid I used whatever was left of your hot water."

She shrugged. "That's okay. As long as there's lightning I wouldn't get in the shower anyway. And without power, we'll just be using cold water regardless."

"True." He took the flashlight and smiled. "Whatever you're making sure smells good. I shouldn't be gone long unless I find a problem."

"Thank you so much for everything."

"My pleasure. It's not like I've done all that much."

And he really didn't feel as if he had, he thought as he climbed the stairs again. Putting up a few tarps had probably done him as much good as it had her.

The springs on the attic stairs squealed their thirst for some oiling as he dropped them and locked them into place. Well, that would be easy enough to fix, he thought. A can of oil and about thirty seconds. He'd take care of that, too.

The ladder was sturdy despite its age. He climbed up

and then crawled out onto some plywood that had been laid over the rafters to protect the ceiling underneath. He crawled along until he ran out of plywood, seeing that nothing was wet, then reached the area were he had tarped the roof. Everything was damp, but he expected that. He didn't see any fresh puddling, and a scan of the tarps overhead didn't expose any water drips. He waited a few minutes, listening to the steady rain drum. It seemed to be okay, but he'd have to check again later. He'd be surprised if there wasn't at least one leaky patch in tarps this old.

But as usual, now that he was looking around, he saw other things that needed doing. There were places where the roof decking looked as if it was starting to pull loose as wood dried and stopped holding the nails. Screws and some glue would be better.

Then he caught himself. Not his house, not his problem. So why the heck was he making a mental checklist?

Maybe because he knew somewhere deep inside he was going to try to help this lady out. He had the time. He had the know-how. He even had the money.

And the thought of leaving her in a tumbling down house in her state sorely troubled him.

When he rejoined her in the kitchen, the aromas were enough to make his stomach growl. Marti had a saucepan simmering on the stove now also, and she stood at the counter cutting fresh broccoli.

She turned, wiping her hands on a bib apron. "Coffee?"

"I'd love some. Just tell me where the cups are."

She pointed to a cabinet and let him serve himself as

she resumed slicing the broccoli. "I hope you like wild rice and broccoli."

"I love both."

She flashed him a smile then went back to work as he sat at the table with his coffee. "How was it up there?"

"Dry so far. Well, dry considering the rain that got in before I could put up the tarps. I'll check again later for leaks." He paused as another thought occurred to him. "I don't know how things work out here. Do you get city water? Or are you on a well?"

"On a well. There's a backup generator for the pump, but that's about all it runs. As long as it holds we won't be without water. Why?"

"Just curious. It struck me you might be on a well out here, but we still had running water."

"My in-laws did something right," she remarked, leaving him to wonder how much they had done wrong. "I'm glad it kicked on, though. I don't know much about it at all. We only needed it once before, and Jeff took care of it."

Jeff, he supposed, was her late husband. "I'll check it out tonight, too. Make sure it's not running out of gas."

"Thank you. I honestly don't know. We have some five-gallon gasoline cans in the pump house, but I don't even know where to fill the generator. I'm just glad it kicked on the way it's supposed to."

A babe in the woods, he thought. Out here in the middle of nowhere, all by herself, and knowing next to nothing about this place. Maybe he could remedy a little of that before he left.

"How long have you been here?" he asked.

"Just six months. It was winter when we got here. I'd just found out I was pregnant."

"I'm sorry about your husband."

"This is going to sound terrible," she said, turning her back as she gave her attention to her cooking, "but I'm not."

That left him utterly flat-footed. He hadn't the least idea how to respond to that. He watched her stir a pot, seeking some appropriate response.

With her butcher knife, she swept the broccoli from the cutting board into another saucepan, added a little water, then started washing her tools. The silence would have seemed deafening except for the endless spattering of rain against the darkening windows.

Finally she joined him at the big old farm table with coffee of her own.

"I told you it would sound awful," she remarked, holding her mug in both hands. "I'm sorry he died, but I'm not sorry he's gone, if you get the difference."

"I get it." He did, but as his thoughts trailed back to Brandy, he realized that, although he didn't miss the constant daily struggle with her depression, he still missed her. There was a difference, but he suspected the difference Marti was talking about wasn't the same as his.

"I don't miss him," she said. "I thought I would, but I don't."

"What happened?"

"When?" Her short laugh held an edge. "He was an alcoholic. When he drank, especially when he drank, he was verbally abusive. Then he lost his job because of it and couldn't get a good enough recommendation to find another. That's when he decided we'd move out here. He'd inherited the house from his parents a couple of years ago, and he was sure we'd be fine. The land was leased every year and he figured we could live on those leases if we were careful. It also prevented him from having to find another job."

"Which was difficult."

"The times are hard. Being an alcoholic makes them harder."

"I imagine it would."

"So we came out here right about the time I realized I was pregnant. I hoped things would get better. I should have known they wouldn't. Not having to sober up to get to work in the morning didn't help. I thought maybe taking the pressure off him might make a difference, but it didn't. If anything, he got worse. Then three months ago he was driving drunk on an icy road." She shook her head. "I may be lonely, but somehow I don't feel as lonely as I did when he was still around."

Before he could react, she seemed to catch herself, giving a quick shake of her head. "Sorry, you didn't need to know all that. I guess it's too easy to talk to a stranger."

"That's okay." He suspected she hadn't talked to anyone about any of this in a long time, if ever. Sometimes you just needed to say things out loud, which was the whole reason he was headed west to see his brother-in-law. To tell Ben the whole story. To get it off his chest with someone else who was grieving. He gathered she didn't have anyone close at all, so why not talk to a stranger? "You've had a rough time of it."

"Others have it worse. I've still got a roof, thanks to you. The rest I can deal with."

"Well, you don't actually have a roof," he reminded her. Then he asked, hesitantly, "Are you in any financial shape to have it repaired?"

"No," she admitted. "I'll figure out something somehow. Right now, after looking at the hay fields, I'm wondering if the people we leased the land to will be able to pay up at the end of the season."

Implied in what she said was that she might be completely broke in a few months.

"I can't do anything about the fields," he said slowly, as feelings warred within him. Part of him was demanding he at least put this woman on a safe footing before he left, and another part of him was demanding he get back on the road before he got tangled up in problems with a size he didn't know. That could be a recipe for a mess for both of them.

But then he made the offer anyway. "I can fix your roof."

"No! Oh no," she said, looking horrified. "I couldn't pay you. I can't buy the materials. But thank you."

He shook his head, wondering if he were losing his mind. Then he remembered how good he'd felt only a few hours ago on her roof, working with his hands again.

"Money isn't an issue for me," he said flatly. "I sold my construction business two months ago. I like working with my hands. In fact, right now I think I need to work with my hands. All I need is a few hot meals and a place to sleep, and I can take care of the roof and maybe a few other things."

"I couldn't ask that." She looked genuinely distressed.

"You're not asking, I'm offering. I'm telling you, Marti, it's been a long time since I felt as good as I did pounding those nails today to put those tarps up. So humor me. Call it my therapy."

"What do you need therapy for?"

"My wife killed herself eight months ago." That was the first time he'd said it that bluntly, and he watched as Marti clapped a hand to her mouth, her blue eyes widening.

"I'm so sorry," she whispered behind her hand.

"Me, too. She suffered from chronic depression. All the docs, all the meds, all the psychiatrists…" He paused. "She finally seemed to be getting better. I came home from work and there she was."

"I can't imagine," she said, her voice thin. She dropped her hand. "I'm so sorry."

"So am I. I'll probably spend the rest of my life wondering how the hell I failed her. But that's neither here nor there. I have to live with it. But fixing your roof would make me feel better about something. Is that too much to ask?"

She stared down at her coffee mug for a long time. He felt the endless minutes tick by.

Finally she looked up at him, her blue eyes damp. "Who's asking whom?" she asked.

"Does it matter? We both have needs, and they seem to mesh. Your roof in exchange for a few days of labor that'll make me feel better. Fair trade?"

At last she nodded. "Fair enough."

Then he forced a smile. "Look out, lady. Construction is my business and my life. I'm going to take over."

At that a fragile smile appeared on her lips. "Have at it," she said. "But only as much as makes you feel good."

Dinner felt like a feast after the way she'd been cooking for herself, although it was nothing really special: roast chicken, seasoned wild rice and buttered broccoli.

She insisted on doing the dishes by herself, even though leaning over the sink now made her back ache a little. Keeping active was getting harder and harder for her as her pregnancy progressed and she had so little she needed to do, living by herself. Yet she knew staying active was essential. She put two kettles on the stove to heat some water for washing and rinsing the dishes, then set to work.

Ryder took the flashlight and headed up to the attic again.

Night had closed in on them. Rain still rattled at the window over the sink, and sometimes she heard the house creak a bit as the wind gusted.

Ryder was going to stay to fix her roof. Amazed that a stranger would make such an offer, her thoughts kept coming back to him. He was a good-looking man, with dark hair and gray cyes and a body that boasted of hard work.

But that was not what impressed her the most. Picking him up to bring him to shelter from the tornado was a small thing, something she would have done for anyone. It cost her nothing but a few seconds of time.

But what he was offering astonished her. To pay for materials and do all that labor in exchange for a bed and some meals? That told her more about him than anything he could have said.

He saw someone in need and stepped up. Not everyone would do that. On the one hand she felt almost guilty for letting him, but on the other she had to admit she needed it, and she hadn't even asked for it.

Wouldn't have dreamed of asking for it.

She almost wanted to cry as she stood there doing dishes. His generosity made her acutely aware of how little generosity she had known since her marriage to Jeff. How little he had taken care of her or cared about her. It was as if Jeff's failures had left an aching hole in her heart, one so big that the kindness of a stranger was almost painful.

She blinked back an unwanted tear, sighed, and kept on washing and scrubbing. Life was what it was. She certainly ought to know that by now. She had plenty of experience of it not being what she wanted, after all.

Except for the baby. Linda Marie was an unexpected blessing, one she looked forward to with the only joy she had felt in a long, long time. Jeff hadn't been happy about it, but at least he hadn't given her hell about being pregnant. Of course, that could have changed with time. She'd only just begun to start showing, really showing, about the time he died. For all she knew, he'd been in denial about the baby.

Wouldn't that have been just like him? He'd been in denial about everything. Every single thing from his drinking to the reasons he could no longer find work.

Yes, she was sorry he was dead, but she didn't really miss him at all.

It was an ugly thought, but it was a truth that had burrowed deep into her heart and mind over the past few months. These days she couldn't even remember if there had ever been any good times with Jeff. Maybe at the beginning. There must have been some back then.

But she couldn't remember them. They were layered over with five years of ugliness, and as far as she was concerned they could stay buried.

She had a different future now, a future that included a new daughter. She needed to keep her attention on that, not the past.

She was wiping the last plate with a towel when she thought of Ryder again. Imagine coming home to find your wife had killed herself. How could you live with that? His words about depression and doctors and medicines indicated that she'd had good care, but evidently it hadn't been enough.

Drying her hands, she thought about that and intuited that at some very deep level, no matter what you had done to try to care for someone, if they committed suicide then you were bound to feel you had failed in some essential way.

No wonder he wanted to pound nails and work on her roof. With demons like that, what other outlet could there be?

She heard him come down the stairs, then he appeared in the kitchen door. She noticed again how attractive he was but pushed the thought away. Now was not the time, and she wasn't sure she'd ever want to become involved with a man again anyway.

"One small, slow leak," he said. "I'll need the biggest pot or bucket you have to make sure it doesn't do any ceiling damage overnight. Other than that, we should be good for now. I'll check again at bedtime to be certain."

She gave him the five-gallon bucket she used for mopping and watched him disappear once again.

The night yawned before her, and she wondered how they would spend the time. No TV, no power. They could talk, become a little better acquainted, but that prospect frightened her a bit.

Did she really want to know him better? What if she started to really like him?

Not that it would matter, she told herself. He'd be leaving as soon as he had fixed the roof. He had said so. He wouldn't want to spend any more time in this godforsaken place than he had to. She wasn't sure she would if she had a choice.

But she didn't have one. Not yet. There was nothing to do but endure.

At least she knew she could do that much.

Ryder went to get the portable radio from the storm shelter so they could try to find some news about the extent of damage around them and when they could expect the weather to clear. He had to detach the antenna that had allowed them to use it in the shelter, but he didn't think he was going to have much trouble aboveground. If he did, he could always find a wire somewhere.

He checked the phone when he returned and found it still out. His cell phone continued to give him no connection. Oh, well, Ben hadn't expected him for a week or two anyway. Tomorrow would be soon enough to give him a call. Ben was already irritated that Ryder was taking the slow route out there. Another few days couldn't matter.

In the meantime, he realized he was grateful to be here. He couldn't imagine that woman being alone and pregnant with no power, no phone, no idea whether roads were passable and nobody to help.

It definitely wasn't right.

She had moved the oil lamps to the living room right off the small entry hall, and he joined her there with the radio. "Do you mind?"

"No. That's a great idea. I was just sitting here wondering what was going on in the rest of the county."

"Maybe we'll find out if I can get a signal. Right now my cell phone thinks the world has vanished."

Her lovely smile reappeared. "It's never easy to get a

cell signal out here. Closer to town they have more towers, but out here where ranches are so spread out, we don't have many. I hear a lot of the ranchers and farmers who can afford them have satellite phones."

But that would be beyond her means, he thought. That didn't sit well with him, either. He supposed in the old days pioneer women had dealt with worse, but this wasn't the old days, this woman didn't much resemble a pioneer with loads of knowledge about how to do things, and a pregnant woman without a reliable telephone struck him as dangerous. But of course he couldn't say so. He'd already inserted himself too much into her life. Maybe more than she wanted.

The radio crackled and the announcer's voice emerged and then disappeared again into the static. Road crews were out trying to clear roads. At one point Marti looked at him.

"I won't be able to get you to town until they clear Eighty-six."

"I'm staying at least a few days anyway."

Bursts of information got through. Line crews from surrounding areas were arriving to help restore power. Conard City had completely lost power. Damage reports remained sketchy as the sheriff's department tried to visit outlying properties. Emergency aid had begun to arrive.

They received an incomplete picture of the situation, some speculation about how many tornadoes and how strong, but the information sufficed to tell Ryder that it was bad. Very bad.

With each bit of news, Marti sagged more. Drawn and pale, she appeared exhausted.

"You need to get to bed," he said finally. "It's been a

stressful day. Let me just check the attic one more time, then you get some sleep. We can assess things better in the morning."

She nodded wordlessly.

He climbed one more time into the attic, checking around, but found no more new leaks. The bucket had hardly filled, so he felt no need to empty it.

Back downstairs, he sent Marti up and watched her climb those stairs as if her feet weighed a ton.

Sympathy squeezed his heart. Unwanted, unwelcome, it happened anyway.

Unbidden, a thought floated across his mind: maybe he could help this woman out in a way he'd never been able to help Brandy. It probably wouldn't ease his sense of guilt much, but it might put a bandage on his soul.

And he so desperately needed a bandage.

Chapter 3

Morning arrived with the kind of perfection that could only follow a serious storm. As long as Ryder didn't look down, all he could see was a sky clear enough and blue enough to hurt the eyes, he felt air so fresh it didn't seem to be able to contain a dust mote, and through the open window he smelled rich earth and green plants. Just outside his window, an untouched tree rustled gently.

Perfect. Until he looked down.

For the first time, without rain and wind lashing him, he saw it all. It spread before him as if the world had been lifted and shaken, then tossed like dice.

From this side of the house he couldn't see the wiped-out hay field, but he could see debris scattered everywhere, some of it large and some of it small, and most of it probably never to be identified again.

Pieces of twisted metal sheeting. Broken boards, scattered tree limbs—some of which, amazingly enough, still had their leaves. An armchair. For God's sake, a chair?

He hated to think of the story behind that chair. Or the ceiling fan that appeared to be in perfect condition about two hundred yards away. Somebody had been hit hard. Had lost everything.

He jammed himself into his clothes and hurried downstairs. He heard stirring from the kitchen, and he couldn't imagine how Marti must be reacting to the sights outside her door. He kind of hoped she hadn't looked out her bedroom window this morning.

Wrapped in a pink terry-cloth robe, she stood at the stove cooking some breakfast sausage. She turned as she heard his footsteps and gave him a wan smile. "You must be hungry. Coffee?"

"Thanks. And I'm starved." He helped himself to a steaming cup of brew, then got out of her way by sitting at the old farm table. "I'm not going to be able to do much about the roof until I can get to town. Any word on that?"

She shook her head. "Eighty-six is still blocked. The…stories on the radio were getting so bad I turned it off. I was lucky, Ryder."

After looking out his window, he had to agree. "Maybe I can find some stuff in the barn to work with. But I took a look outside… There's plenty to do out there, Marti."

"I know." Her hand shook a little as she turned the sausage. "I saw. Some of it anyway. I don't even know where to begin. People lost their entire houses."

He'd already figured that out. "Let me think about it," he suggested. "There's cleanup, and there are things

I want to check out about the rest of the house. The way things were flying, there might be more damage than just the roof. Anyway, like I said, plenty to do."

"Eggs?" she asked as she forked sausage from the pan.

"Please."

"How many and how do you want them?"

"Three, please, over easy." The way he planned to work today, he figured fat would fuel him more than it would harm him.

At last she joined him at the table with her own single egg and a slice of toast. In front of him she put a plate with another four slices. He dug in. Simple food, but good food and plenty of it. He just hoped she was eating enough and not going hungry in order to feed him. But he couldn't figure out how to ask without offending her.

Then she answered without being asked. "I can't eat much in the mornings," she remarked. "Morning sickness is supposed to go away, but mine hasn't."

He looked up from his plate. "Really? That's awful. Is something wrong?"

"I'm perfectly healthy." She managed a smile as she lifted her piece of toast. "At least it goes away by noon. But that's why I haven't even dressed yet."

"You look fine to me in terry cloth." The words popped out unbidden, and he saw her start. Then she blushed. "Sorry," he said swiftly. "That was out of line."

"No, no," she said hastily. "I was feeling like a hag, but I'm not anymore."

Again he caught sight of her enchanting smile. It made him feel good. He'd like to see a whole lot more of that smile. Then it struck him that getting attached to seeing her smile might not be good for either of them.

He had to get on to Fresno soon. He'd promised Ben, and he knew Ben needed to talk about Brandy as much as he did.

But for now he had to leave this woman in somewhat better shape, and he had to do it without making either of them regret his eventual departure.

So he turned businesslike. "I want to check the barn and find out what's in there. Maybe I can find materials for repairs, at least temporary ones. I saw some debris in your yard that I think I'd better clean up so it doesn't blow around and cause more damage if you have another storm. I'll get started as soon as I'm done eating."

Her smile had faded at his change of tone and he felt a bit like a beast.

"You don't have to do all that," she protested.

He shrugged. "Lady, there are just some things a decent man needs to do, okay?"

She didn't argue with that. At her insistence he left her with the dishes, then headed out toward the barn. He'd gotten used to having space over the past few weeks, and all of a sudden he was feeling crowded. How stupid was that?

But it was a relief to walk into the barn and be alone. Sometimes a man just needed room to think. Unfortunately, his thoughts kept wanting to turn to Marti. He decided to let them. Brandy had occupied his every waking moment for years now. Maybe he just needed a break.

And maybe, just possibly, he was entitled to it.

He opened up every door and window in the barn to let in the morning light and discovered a treasure trove that hadn't been apparent late yesterday by the light of a single flashlight.

Someone had once worked this ranch, evidently,

although for what he was no real judge. There were a few horse stalls, some tack in the back room, some power equipment and a load of odds and ends that might come in handy. Whatever this had all once been, it was obvious it had been neglected for a long time. Layers of dust coated everything, and rust covered a lot of the steel.

Then, looking up, he saw sunlight peeking through holes in the roof. A total mess from a construction standpoint alone. This barn had obviously weathered a good many decades, but if it didn't get repaired soon, it wouldn't weather many more. Some creeping vines had even begun to grow inside, evidently getting enough water and light from the holes above.

He sighed. He hated to see a building neglected this way. Then he reminded himself that his task was to make sure Marti was safe in her home and that some random thunderstorm wouldn't deprive her of her only shelter. The rest of it wasn't his business.

He cleared space to pile the debris as he recovered it then set to work, all the while wondering how she would get this stuff trucked out of here. Because it was going to take a truck.

He thought of using the tractor that was under a sort of lean-to outside the barn but then dismissed the idea. He didn't know how much of that stuff growing out there was someone's crop, and although he definitely had to get rid of the debris, he didn't want to cost Marti any income because he'd wiped out huge chunks of someone's hay or whatever.

As he worked under the steadily warming sun, carting handfuls and armloads of crap to the barn, it struck him how out of his element he was here. It was halfway to moving to another planet, he thought. He knew how to fix her house, how to fix her barn, but he had no idea what was growing in those fields, how much it might mean to someone and how much tromping it could take.

He started to feel worse with nearly every step he took, wondering if the crushed stalks would revive. Nor was it as if he could stick to a single path. The tornado had not been so obliging.

When Marti called him for lunch, he went upstairs to wash up and took the opportunity to look out all the windows again. As far as he could see, there was more twisted metal, more wood, wire...and that was just what he could see in the tall growth. *Hell.*

Marti had dressed in jeans and a bright-blue maternity top that brought out the blue of her eyes. She had made him two thick chicken sandwiches and more coffee. On her own plate was a single sandwich and beside it a glass of milk.

"I need to know some things," he said as he joined her.

"Like what?"

"Like what's growing out there, how much trampling it can stand and whether I should just leave some of the debris. It's scattered everywhere, but I know damn-all about farming."

"It's hay around the house," she said. "Truthfully? They won't be able to mow it if there's much debris out there."

"So the crop would be wasted if I don't clear it?"

"I think so. If the phone was working, I could call the guy who leased the land and ask him, to be sure. I don't know much more about it than you do, Ryder, except I'm pretty sure the mowers would get beat up if they suck up debris and try to bail it."

"Most likely. And it would probably kill the mower blades."

"Why do you ask?"

"Because I'm trying to save as much of the crop as I can by pulling stuff out by hand. But there's a lot of stuff out there."

"Then the crop is lost." The corners of her mouth pulled down. "You can't do all that work."

"I can do it. Someone has to because if it's left there you won't be able to grow hay next year for the same reason."

Her eyes widened a bit, then she put her forehead in her hand. "God," she whispered almost inaudibly, "it just keeps getting worse."

"Don't think that way," he said, maybe a little sharply. "Just don't think that way. There's always a solution."

Her head jerked up. He'd startled her and felt badly about it. "I'm sorry, I didn't mean to snap."

She didn't answer immediately, then astonished him. "You must have heard a lot of that from your wife."

He really didn't want to go there. Unfortunately, she was right. There had been times when Brandy's inability to see hope, or see a solution, or just deal with something had nearly driven him up the wall. He had understood she was sick and couldn't help it, and he'd bitten back more irritation than he could even remember, but sometimes it had gotten to him even though he never voiced it.

But now he had voiced it, and worse, he had voiced it to a woman who didn't deserve it.

"I'm sorry," he said again. "You're right. I wasn't reacting to you."

She gave a little shrug and picked up her sandwich.

"I read somewhere the hardest part of moving on is that you keep reacting through old filters that might not apply. When you first said that, I reacted to Jeff. So I guess you have a right to react to your wife."

He studied her as she chewed and swallowed. "This is going to be fun," he said after a few moments without any humor at all.

"How so?" she asked.

"We're both full of mines. God help us."

She astonished him with a little laugh. "Indeed. But it's only until you can move on. A few days, right? I think we can manage."

"It might be easier if we had Kevlar vests."

At that her laughter became full-throated. "If they make one to fit a heart, I don't know about it. But I promise to check my responses."

"Me, too," he agreed. "The thing is, I never said a thing like that to my wife. So where the hell did it come from?"

"Maybe," she suggested, "you're dealing with a lot of pent-up stuff. I know I am. Sometimes it's just easier to express to a stranger, someone your heart isn't already tied up in knots with."

She had a point, but that didn't make it right. Then she spoke tentatively.

"It must have been hard to live with someone who was so depressed."

That went straight to the heart of it. He hesitated, not sure he wanted to share much, then realizing that this whole journey he was on was about trying to understand. Maybe talking about it with someone who wasn't involved could kick him a little further down that road.

"The hard part," he said, "was that I couldn't make

her happy. I couldn't fix her. I couldn't do a damn thing except make sure she got good doctors and good therapy and took her meds. I have to admit, it was years before I finally accepted it. Although sometimes I wonder if I really have. Her docs told me. Hell, even Brandy told me that I wasn't in any way responsible for her depression, and there wasn't a damn thing I could do about it. But you never stop hoping. Never stop feeling that if you could just find the right thing to say or do, she'd be happy, even if only for a little while."

"I'm sorry," she said quietly.

"I admit, I'm a fixer. I see something wrong, I want to straighten it out. I couldn't do that for my wife. There were times when she'd get better. Times when she could laugh or enjoy things, but then the pain would come back. What bothers me sometimes is I could never imagine that pain. Never understand how it could be so big and so consuming. Never imagine how it could hurt so much to just be alive."

She caught him by surprise, reaching out to cover one of his work-roughened hands with her soft and delicate one. His eyes started to feel hot, but he battled down the grief. "It just was, Marti. That's all I can say. It just was. And I'm still trying to understand how one day she could seem almost happy, and the next she could kill herself. I wonder if that happiness wasn't just an illusion, a relief of some kind because she'd already made up her mind she was going to end it. I'll never know."

"I am so, so sorry."

He just shook his head, uncomfortable with how he had just spilled his guts. How had it helped? Saying it out loud hadn't answered the questions. He was beginning to think there were no answers at all, anywhere.

"So you said you were going to Fresno?" she said, clearly trying to change the subject.

"To see Brandy's brother, Ben. He has lots of questions, too."

"Why didn't you just fly?"

"Because I needed some time inside my own head. God knows what I'm going to tell him."

"Why should you have to tell him anything? He must have known how sick Brandy was."

Ryder looked at her grimly. "I get the feeling he thinks I didn't do enough. Or that I did something wrong. Can't blame him for that, can I? Let me get back to work."

He rose, leaving one sandwich untouched, and headed back to the fields. Hard work was his only salvation.

Marti watched him go, surprised by the depth of sorrow she felt for him. She had thought she had quit feeling some time ago—at least with regard to anything except the coming baby.

She placed her hands protectively over her stomach, enjoying that connection with the future, then wrapped his sandwich in some plastic wrap. He hadn't eaten nearly enough, she was sure, and would probably want it for a snack.

He did seem like a fixer, she thought as she puttered with household chores. Heck, look what he was doing around here, refusing to leave her to deal with her problems on her own.

Part of her felt guilty about that, but after listening to him at lunch, it struck her that it might be good therapy for him, to be able to help someone in need. To just feel useful to a woman who couldn't help herself.

That eased her independent streak a bit. But as she tried to think what his marriage must have been like for him, the only parallel she could draw was Jeff.

Jeff had been alcoholic. Back before they'd moved out here, she'd gone to some meetings for families of alcoholics to try to understand and had simply come away feeling badly about herself. Was she somehow enabling him? She'd never been able to answer that question to her own satisfaction. She didn't encourage his drinking. She frowned upon it. When she had been able to, she'd often just left when he was drunk and gone to stay with a friend. What was left? Divorce?

The thought had certainly crossed her mind. But every time it did, he'd dry out for a while and things would get better. Almost as if he had a radar, she thought ruefully.

But he'd taken a toll on her, too, she realized in retrospect. Little by little he had chipped away at her self-confidence until she questioned her every judgment. Even while he was digging at her, cratering her sense of self-worth, he'd tell her how much he loved her and needed her.

Then there were those damn marriage vows: for better or worse, in sickness and in health. She hadn't taken those vows lightly, ever. Each and every time she had considered divorce, it had seemed like breaking a solemn oath and admitting failure.

Never in her life had she broken a promise. Her father had raised her to believe her word was her bond and the only measure of her integrity. Bailing out on the most important vow of her life had struck her as the worst thing she could possibly do. Each time she had seriously contemplated it, she had wondered how she would ever live with herself again.

Then Jeff had died, and after the first shock all she had been able to feel was relief. Maybe that was ugly, but there it was: truth. She had been relieved.

Loathsome though it was, she accepted it. That was how she felt, and no crocodile tears were about to change that. She might feel guilty for feeling that way, but guilt couldn't change it.

It had to be very different for Ryder. She gathered he had struggled hard to find a way to help his wife back to health and that losing her had not relieved him. Far from it. He seemed to feel responsible in some way. Apparently from what little he had said, Brandy's brother was helping that feeling along.

She wondered if it was wise for him to go see Ben, but she pushed the thought away. None of her business. Ryder had to do what Ryder had to do.

Just as she did. She climbed the stairs to the small nursery she had been trying to make. It was a poor attempt. With so little money, all she really had was a traveling bassinet that would work for a few months and a dresser set up for a changing table. Dreams of wallpaper and paint and a full-size crib with mobiles remained just that: dreams.

Someday, she promised herself. After the baby was born and she could find a job. Then she'd make a room that would tell Linda Marie how loved she truly was.

Until then she could only stand in the doorway, look at the few things she had been able to prepare and finally walk in and look at one of the impossibly small T-shirts and the incredibly tiny booties. She couldn't imagine even an infant fitting into something so small.

She hugged a shirt to herself and closed her eyes, letting herself dream, however briefly, of a better future.

Ryder worked like a demon all afternoon, until his muscles ached and fatigue settled into his very bones. Just as he was dragging the last piece of twisted metal into the barn, he heard a vehicle.

Turning, he saw a sheriff's vehicle pulling up, a tan SUV with a clearly painted star on the side and light rack on the roof. He dropped the metal, brushed his palms on his jeans and headed that way, glad to see somebody had finally gotten through to check on Marti.

The deputy climbed out, watching his approach, and something in his stance made Ryder acutely aware that he was a stranger in a place that probably didn't see a whole lot of strangers.

The officer was tall, well over six feet, with long black hair that held a few streaks of gray. No mistaking the guy's indigenous roots.

"Hi," Ryder said, approaching slowly, hoping he looked relaxed and open.

"Howdy," came the response. "I don't remember seeing you around before."

"I just got here in time for a huge tornado. Marti— Ms. Chastain—offered me shelter and I hung around to help out."

"Got some ID?"

Ryder reached into his hip pocket and pulled out a wallet. He flipped it open and handed it to the deputy.

"Just the license, please."

So Ryder pulled out his license and passed it over.

Eyes as black as obsidian scanned it then looked up. "Long way from home."

"I'm heading for Fresno to see family. I decided to take the scenic route."

The deputy nodded. "Hold on and stand back."

Cripes, Ryder thought. They really weren't used to strangers around here. But then he thought of Marti, of a pregnant widow all alone, which probably everyone knew, and decided the deputy might have cause.

He watched as the man half-slipped onto his car seat and picked up his radio. He heard his information go out to a dispatcher who sounded like an aging bullfrog.

The deputy returned but held on to the license. "Not trying to be unfriendly," the man said. "I'm Micah Parish. We're just careful around here, Mr. Kelstrom."

"Be my guest. I take it the road is clear now? I promised Marti I'd fix her roof before I move on."

"I had to do some four-wheeling to get here. You might have another day or so before you can get to town. But I'd better warn you, supplies are selling out fast. They're hoping to get in another truckload of shingles and plywood tomorrow or the next day."

Ryder nodded. "How bad is it? We're getting spotty reports on the radio." He turned and pointed out toward the bare earth path left by the twister. "You can see how close we came."

"Yeah, I've been seeing that path on and off for miles. You were lucky. In fact, a lot of people were, mainly because we're so spread out. Most of the damage is repairable, but a couple of ranchers lost their homes. Totally gone. Lots of roof damage, wind damage, hail damage, flying debris damage. I guess altogether we had four tornadoes touch down."

"My God."

Parish nodded. "Then, of course, it might take a week

to get power fully restored. We never got around in these parts to putting the lines underground. Poles are down everywhere. We're lucky we got phone service back in town."

Ryder gave him a rueful smile. "Maybe you ought to put those lines underground when you repair them."

At that he got a faint smile in return. "It's being talked about, believe me. The thing is, tornadoes are rare around here, so we're going to be arguing about whether we can afford the expense when it might be another five or ten years before we see something like that again."

The radio squawked, then the froggy-voiced dispatcher said, "He's clean, Micah. His prints are on file for licensing purposes as a general contractor in the state of New York."

"Thanks, Velma." Micah keyed off the radio and returned Ryder's license. "Welcome to Conard County."

"I already had a helluva welcome when Marti picked me up and saved me from a tornado."

Micah chuckled. "That's some how-de-do, I admit. Is Marti around?"

"Inside, I think. I was just getting ready to call it a day. Mind if I tag along?"

"Not at all. What were you doing?"

"There's debris all over the place. I was worried a storm might pick it up and cause more damage. Then Marti told me those hayfields will be worthless if they're full of debris."

Micah nodded. "Nobody can mow it that way."

"Unless they want to do it by hand. I don't know how much this mess will cost her in terms of her leases, but

I wouldn't feel good leaving her in no shape to lease the land again next year."

Micah paused and looked at him. "Do you know Marti?"

"Just met her."

Micah seemed to measure him all over again. "Do-gooder?"

"Fixer. And right now fixing anything feels good."

Micah gave a slight nod and they resumed walking toward the house. "This woman needs some help, but she's never asked for any. Probably shy, being new to the area and all. But right now, there isn't a lot of help available."

"I wouldn't think so."

"We do keep an eye on everyone, though, new or not."

There was no mistaking the warning. Ryder took it in good part. Parish didn't know him, after all, but more importantly he was glad that somebody besides him in this county cared about Marti, whether she knew it or not.

"I'm actually glad to hear that," he said frankly. "The picture she was painting of her isolation had me worried."

"She is isolated. Some by being new, some caused by that idiot husband of hers, some by simple distance. It's not the best place for a pregnant woman to be alone."

"Then maybe we need to get her to be more sociable."

At that Micah smiled. "Might work. Folks'll welcome her if they feel she wants to be welcomed. But if a body wants to be standoffish, they'll respect that, too. Maybe I'll ask Faith to run by when the roads are clear."

"Faith?"

"My wife. The wonderful mother of my two sets of twins as well as an older daughter."

"Sounds like she has her hands full."

Micah shook his head. "Twins. You'd think one set would be enough, wouldn't you?" But there was humor in his voice. "Thank God they're getting older. When they were babies I thought neither of us would ever sleep again."

"How old are they now?"

"Youngest set is eleven. Next are fourteen. Then we've got a seventeen-year-old daughter."

Ryder, who had almost no experience with children, could hardly imagine a house that full. Not that he objected. He actually thought it sounded appealing.

He opened the front door for Micah, calling out for Marti.

"Deputy Parish is here to check on you."

Marti appeared at the top of the stairs and began to make her slow way down. For the first time Ryder wondered how much the baby affected her balance. All of a sudden those stairs didn't look safe to him.

But she made it and reached them with a warm smile. That smile that Ryder thought lit up the world.

"Deputy," she said. "How nice. The rest of the world still exists? Can I get you some coffee?"

"Just call me Micah, ma'am. And I'd love that coffee. I've been on and off the road all day checking up on folks."

Marti bustled around the kitchen making coffee, looking more cheerful than she had yet. Apparently it made her feel good that someone had come to check on her when she'd been feeling so alone. Or maybe she just liked the opportunity to do something for someone.

They gathered around the table waiting for the coffee and Marti asked the same question Ryder had. "How bad is it?"

"I was telling Ryder here that you won't be able to get into town for a few days yet. A lot of roads are still blocked. And you won't have power for up to maybe a week. So what I'm here to find out is, do you have enough food, enough gas and so on? I take it since you have running water you've got a generator?"

"Yes," Marti said. "I'm not sure how much gas it has, but I think it only kicks on when I need the well pump."

Ryder shook his head. "There's about twenty gallons of gas out there, and the generator idles when the pump isn't running. I don't know if twenty gallons will get her through more than a few days."

Micah nodded and pulled out a small notebook. "Okay, you need gas. What about refrigeration?"

"Everything's thawing," Marti admitted. "I'm going to need to throw a lot of stuff away soon, unless we get power."

"Maybe I can run a cable from the generator to your freezer," Ryder said. "If I can find an appropriate cord."

"We'll check that out," Micah said, "before I leave. If necessary I can be back tonight with essentials. Anything else, assuming it'll be two days minimum before you can get to town? And keeping in mind that there's been enough disruption that supplies are short there, too. I mean, most of the groceries have had to dump the contents of their coolers."

Ryder saw Marti almost sag as the dimensions of the destruction came home yet again. "If I can save what's in my freezer," she said quietly, "we'll be okay for a week. ·

I just went shopping the day before, and I always shop for a couple of weeks at a time. But if we can't save it..."

While the coffee finished perking, Micah and Ryder went out to the pump house to check things out.

"This generator should be able to handle a freezer," Ryder said, examining the label on the side. "The water pump, the freezer, maybe a few other things if she needs them. But I'm going to need weatherproof cords to run to the house. I haven't seen any around."

"Okay, tell her to keep that fridge closed and I'll be back in a few hours. I know where to get some cords. My place."

"How is your place?" Ryder asked, suddenly realizing he'd expressed no concern for the deputy or his family.

"We live so far out I have plenty of generator capacity of my own. Had the thing hardwired years ago because it was getting so every blizzard left us in the dark. No, we're fine. But unless I can be sure the two of you are going to be okay, I'm taking you out of here."

But where to? Ryder wondered as he watched the deputy drive away. It sounded like this was a bigger mess than he'd even begun to imagine.

"He left?"

Marti's voice called him back and he turned to see her on the porch. "He's gone to get some cords so I can run power to your fridge from the generator. He'll be back."

"He didn't even have his coffee."

"Keep it warm." Ryder tried a smile. "He'll be back, and then he'll probably be ready for a whole pot."

"He's a nice man," she said. "He was the one who came to tell me about Jeff's accident. I would have liked to do something nice for him, even if it's only coffee."

"You'll get your chance," Ryder promised her. He

joined her on the porch and opened the door, suggesting they go inside. As evening closed around them, the air was getting chilly. "And I'd like some of that coffee right now."

She led the way into the kitchen but didn't object when he motioned her to a seat and poured coffee for both of them. He lit one of the oil lamps and placed it on the edge of the table away from them.

"We need to make a list of what you'll need for the next few days," he said. "If stuff in your fridge has been getting warm, then we can't afford to overlook milk and things like that. You must need your milk."

"The baby does," she agreed. "I have calcium supplements that I could take but they make my stomach hurt. I'd rather drink milk."

"Got a pad somewhere?"

She pointed to the fridge. He went to get it, grabbing a pencil from a magnetic cup beside it. "Okay, milk. Enough for a few days at least. Micah's already making a list for us and if he's willing to bring us gas, I bet he's willing to bring you milk."

"I hate to impose..."

He looked at her. "Sometimes, Marti, it just feels good to do something for someone else. I think you know that."

She sighed then smiled faintly. "I'm not doing too good at the whole independent woman thing right now."

"Of course not. Your roof has been damaged and your yard looks like Paul Bunyan went through in a hurry. Not many people could deal with that solo. If any. So quit feeling badly about needing help."

She gave him another small smile then fell silent. When she spoke again, it was to change the subject.

"I have a whole bunch of stuff starting to thaw in the freezer, but I'm not sure any of it will thaw in time to cook. I'm sorry, but I didn't even think of dinner. I've fallen out of the habit of cooking every night."

"I'm sure there's something we can manage. Don't worry about it."

"But you worked hard all day. And we ate the last of the chicken at lunch. You need to eat."

"I'm not the only one who needs to eat. You've got a passenger, lady. We should be worrying about you first."

"I've still got one of your lunch sandwiches wrapped up. You could eat that."

He just shook his head. No way was he going to eat and leave her hungry. He could go a night without food, no problem. She was in a different category.

He popped up from the table. "Mind if I invade your pantry?"

"Go ahead. Help yourself."

While he wasn't exactly a chef, Brandy's illness had taught him how to cook—otherwise they both might have starved for long periods or been reduced to take-out, which wasn't always the healthiest thing. So he figured he'd find something he could patch together into a meal without a big problem.

Once in the pantry, though, he froze, suddenly caught in a wave of grief. Brandy. How much he'd had to take care of her and in the end it hadn't helped her at all.

Sometimes it hurt so freaking bad he couldn't stand it. Then he thought of the woman out there he was trying to help and wondered if he wasn't doing the same thing all over again.

Or maybe he was just doing penance. God knew he needed it.

Chapter 4

Micah returned before darkness had fully settled over the county. By flashlight, he worked with Ryder to bring some power to the refrigerator and offered him a few more cords to hang on to in case they needed some other power.

The humming of the refrigerator sounded loud, Marti thought, after it had been silent for more than twenty-four hours. She was relieved to hear it come on, although she suspected it was probably too late for the milk and some other things. She began to pull them out for the trash or to pour down the sink.

On the counter was an assortment of things Ryder had pulled from the pantry and the fridge: carrots, lentils, cabbage, onions…a whole lot of stuff that looked like it might make a good soup. She glanced at the clock, though, and wondered how late they would eat.

Before she could decide to start cooking, she heard the tromp of booted feet and turned to see Micah coming in with an ice chest and Ryder on his heels with a big box.

"Just some stuff Faith sent to get you through a few days," Micah said.

"But can you spare it?"

Micah just looked at her. "We have five kids. Do you think Faith would send anything if it would leave the kids hungry?"

Some reluctance in Marti let go and she laughed. "No, I guess not."

It wasn't enough food to make her feel awful about it, but it was the right amount to make her feel grateful. Milk, some butter and other perishables, and in the box some bread and peanut butter and a crock full of stew.

"Stew's from last night," Micah remarked as he at last sipped a cup of the coffee she had made for him. "Just pop it in your oven for an hour, she said. And she said to thank you for taking it because there's not enough to make another meal for seven, and getting the kids to eat leftovers otherwise is impossible." He winked. "And I'd like to thank you, too, because much as I like her stew, eating it every day for lunch for a week or more gets to be bit much."

Marti released the last bit of her tension about the generosity and sat at the table with the two men until Micah announced he needed to get moving. "More places to check on," he explained. "I'll be back tomorrow with some gas for the generator." With him he took the list that Ryder and Marti had barely put together.

Night was creeping in, and a single oil lamp did little

to hold it at bay. She studied Ryder across the table as delicious aromas began to emerge from the oven.

He looked tired, she thought. As well he should be. But there was something else. She had noticed a change in him after he went to the pantry. He'd seemed to stay in there awfully long to look for just a handful of items, and when he had emerged, something had changed.

He seemed more withdrawn. Perhaps even sad. Was he thinking about Brandy? She would willingly have listened to him talk about his late wife, but she wasn't sure bringing it up would be the wise thing to do. Maybe it would just be better to leave him alone with his demons.

"You know," she said suddenly, "I've become a wimp."

That startled him. All of a sudden he was totally focused on her, and that focus nearly took her breath away. She'd noted before that he was an attractive man, but it hadn't struck her before how amazingly good his full attention felt. Places inside her that hadn't felt warm in a very long time grew warm. In fact, some of them became instantly hot. She hoped he couldn't see her blush.

"Why in the hell do you think you're a wimp?" he asked her almost roughly.

She was startled by his tone and almost folded in on herself. But just in time she caught the response and reminded herself this wasn't Jeff. "Because I second-guess everything I think or might say."

He tilted his head a little. "Jeff?"

She nodded. "I always had a leash on my tongue. And I couldn't even make up my mind to divorce him."

"So unleash your tongue. The divorce question is moot now, don't you think?"

That made her laugh a little. "Most certainly. Did you ever think about divorce?"

As soon as she asked it, she wished the words unsaid. She had an urge to cut out her own tongue. His entire face, handsome and full of strength, seemed to melt and sag a little.

"Sometimes," he whispered. "Sometimes. Hell."

After a few moment she murmured, "You're only human."

"Yeah, I know. I really do get that. It's just that..." He hesitated. "I guess human wasn't good enough."

"Don't say that."

"Why not? It's true. Not for Brandy. Not that she ever berated me—because she didn't. Bless her, she spent a whole lot of time telling me it wasn't my fault she was sick. Her doctors even told me. But she was still my responsibility and I couldn't help her. And sometimes I got tired of trying constantly and still watching her curl up in a ball and just cry. Sometimes I felt like heading out and never coming back because, damn it, I just couldn't make it any better and I always wondered if I was making it worse. Believe me, I'm no saint."

"Maybe you expected too much of yourself."

"Probably. I've been accused of that." He sighed. "She wasn't depressed when we met. It didn't get bad until after the first year. And then it got really bad. At first I had trouble even understanding. Maybe I still do. I don't have a reference point for hurting so badly for no reason at all that life is intolerable. I have a blind spot. Never been there, never done that. I couldn't understand why nothing could cheer her up, nothing could make her happy. Couldn't understand how she could be too tired to even get out of bed, how she could say things about buying a gun or slashing her wrists. Although I guess I'm glad she did say them because then I was able to race her to a hospital. Then we got on the treatment treadmill. Or maybe a better description would be a treatment roller coaster. They must have tried every antidepressant in the books. She'd get better for a little while—not top-of-the-world better, but functional—and then crash again. They even tried shock treatments. God, that was scary. That made her forgetful in ways that seriously worried me, although I was warned to expect it. But not even that did the trick. Finally a new drug came out. It seemed to be working. I thought Brandy was coming back."

"But instead she went away."

"For good." He passed a hand over his face, then leaned back. "I guess she's not hurting anymore."

"I'm sure she's not, but she sure left you a world of pain."

"Suicide does that," he said flatly. "Even her own brother…" He stopped himself.

"Ben doesn't hold you responsible, does he? How could he? Doesn't he understand she was sick?"

"Sometimes I think he does, and sometimes I'm not so sure. Anyway, he's got as much crap to deal with as I do about Brandy. She left a whole lot of question marks behind her."

He fell silent and she let him be. She figured she had already stirred up his demons enough.

"Ben's an okay guy," he said presently. "He just didn't see her illness up close and personal the way I did. So I figure we'll talk until we make some kind of peace with it. I don't think we'll ever get that closure everyone talks about, but we've both got to learn to live with it. Her sickness killed her as surely as if it was cancer. That's the hard part to get."

"I'm sure it must be."

He looked at her again, giving her the faintest of smiles. "Sorry. That was a downer."

"I brought it up. I guess I'm lucky. My husband killed himself, too, if you want to look at it that way. I'm just glad he didn't kill anyone else in the process. He made a stupid decision, to drive drunk. But if it hadn't been that, he probably would have killed his liver before long."

"He was drinking that much?"

"Constantly. Maybe it was a different version of what happened to Brandy. People don't feel a whole lot of sympathy for alcoholics, either. It's a disease, an addiction. Like you, I tried to help. But with alcoholics, there's really only one person who can do it. One doc tried to get him to take that medicine that makes you sick if you drink but he wouldn't. And without a run-in with the police, nobody was going to make him do anything."

She shook her head. "Sorry. But sometimes I used to wish he'd get a DUI so they'd send him to rehab. Unfortunately, the one time turned out to be the last time."

"So neither of us are wearing halos?"

The dryness of his tone caught her by surprise, and a chuckle escaped. "I guess not," she admitted and felt again that warm, full-bodied sense of attraction. Amazing—she hadn't felt like a truly sexual being in years, not even the night Linda Marie had been conceived. Then she'd felt used.

So she could still look at a man and respond as a woman? That felt good and she tucked it away inside. He couldn't possibly see her that way himself, not when she was so pregnant, but even so she didn't mind feeling the response to him. It meant she was still alive, that she might someday have a real life again. A real life for her and her baby.

Just then Linda Marie kicked hard and she jumped. Her hand flew to her belly. "Wow. She could have put that ball through the goal posts."

Ryder suddenly laughed. "Would it be okay for me to feel it? I've never felt a baby kick inside the womb."

"Sure." She smiled and waved him around the table. Then she took her hand and placed it on her firm belly. How warm and big he felt.

"Just wait," she said. "Linda doesn't do command performances, but she seems to be awake now."

"Does it hurt?"

"Almost never. Once in a while she seems to find a sensitive place, but that's rare. Mostly it just feels like little pokes."

Then Linda Marie obliged with a kick, almost as if she felt the warmth from Ryder's big hand.

"Oh, wow," he breathed, and his face brightened. "Oh, wow. It felt like a tiny foot."

"Maybe it was. Sometimes I can almost see it but not usually. I can feel it when she turns over, too."

He waited a few more minutes, but the baby was evidently done for now. He returned to his seat, looking awed. "That is so amazing," he said and smiled. "Phenomenal! Thanks."

"It is pretty amazing," she admitted, rubbing her tummy with her palms. "I love it when she's active because I'm sure everything's okay. I hate it when she gets quiet for too long."

"I can imagine." His whole demeanor had lightened

and she was thankful for the distraction the baby had provided.

"I feel blessed," she said after a moment. "I guess I am. This pregnancy is a blessing, and somehow I'll deal with the rest of it. I kind of have to."

He nodded, his expression growing thoughtful. "Well," he said after a few moments, "I've got some time, so before I leave I'll make sure you don't have a whole lot of big things to worry about."

"Ryder…"

He held up his hand. "Please. Don't argue. I need the work, I need to do something useful. You'll be doing me a favor."

She hesitated, then asked, "If work is so important to you, why did you sell your business?"

"That's complicated." He rose and refilled their coffee mugs. The aroma coming from the oven was growing more enticing with each minute.

"You don't have to tell me," she hastened to say.

"It's complicated but it's not tough," he said a bit dryly. "Not some mega-emotional upheaval, although what happened may have helped it along. I got into the business working as a framer."

She nodded as he sat across from her again.

"Hands-on. I still love the smell of freshly cut lumber. Anyway, with time I moved up, developed more skills, got more responsibility. About the time I met Brandy I'd become a GC, a general contractor, the guy who organizes everything and then supervises. From there it was a relatively small step to setting up my own business as a GC. Unfortunately, over the years, the job became less hands-on. Other people were doing the work I loved while I was in a mess of paperwork and business-related stuff. It didn't seem so important because Brandy was keeping me pretty busy. Going to work was one way I took care of her needs. But after she was gone…" He shrugged. "It felt hollow. I wasn't doing any of the stuff I loved doing. None of it. So finally I decided I needed a new start. Maybe I was trying to escape."

Again she kept her response to a nod, afraid of silencing him.

"I don't know exactly. I just know I needed to stop feeling so hollow. I couldn't get Brandy back but maybe I could get back to doing what I loved. I was even thinking about getting into cabinetry, really highly skilled carpentry, and I couldn't do that with the business hanging around my neck. It took me a couple of months to sell after I made the decision, and then I decided to take this break and go talk with Ben. It was clear he was as messed up about the whole situation as I was, and I thought maybe if we got together things might settle a bit for us both."

"I hope they will."

He sighed. "I don't know. But working on your roof yesterday reminded me how much I absolutely love to work with my hands. So if you don't mind, I'm going to indulge myself around here. You could say this opportunity is God-sent for me—if you don't find that callous of me, that is."

She thought about that. "I don't find it callous," she said. "That tornado was going to come through, regardless. So maybe you were God-sent for me, too."

Then she smiled. She had to admit she liked the way he responded, with a slow-growing smile of his own, one that reached his gray eyes and crinkled the corners. Man, he was handsome, with cleanly chiseled features and a slightly weathered face. He was sun bronzed and healthy-looking, and his entire body boasted the compact strength of someone who worked hard. She liked that, especially after Jeff, who had looked neither healthy nor hard-working the last couple of years.

Then she saw a light in those eyes she would have found unmistakable years ago, before Jeff had made her feel so unattractive. Surely he couldn't be responding to her, too? Not when she was so big with child?

For just a few seconds she allowed herself to entertain the thought, allowed herself to feel the first delicious stirrings of sexual awareness, then she stepped down on it. It would do her no good to let something like that grow. He was going to move on to Fresno in a few days, and she had no business even thinking about something that could only sadden her one way or another.

No attachments. Not now. And certainly not when they would be so ephemeral.

"I wish I could help more," she said, trying to get her mind off the acute sensitivity that seemed to want to grow between her legs.

"Lady, you're helping me plenty by letting me get back into practice around here. Damn, it feels good."

This time he insisted on doing the dishes while she put her feet up in the living room. He set an oil lamp on the table beside her, telling her frankly that she looked worn out and asking if pregnant women weren't supposed to get some rest.

She would have hated to tell him just how much rest she had taken that afternoon while he'd been laboring so mightily to clear her fields. Inevitably, she'd taken a nap, so she shouldn't be feeling tired at all.

But it felt good to be pampered, and her ankles had

swollen a little bit, so she didn't argue when he pulled the old hassock over for her and waited until she put her feet on in. Then he brought her a cup of fresh herbal tea and disappeared into the kitchen.

The sounds that emanated from that direction made her smile. She listened to him talk to himself a bit as he figured out that he needed to boil water, and then he started humming.

Darn, he even had a nice baritone and good pitch. She let her head fall back and closed her eyes and tried not to wish that she could know moments like this into the indefinite future.

But this was how it was supposed to feel, wasn't it, in a good relationship? She wouldn't know from experience. She tried to remember even one time that Jeff had coddled her this way and couldn't. Not one.

She dozed off as she had insane visions of many more evenings just like this one. It didn't matter that her house was falling apart, that the fields might be ruined, that there might be no money come harvest time. If she could just have more and more evenings like this one...

When she awoke, Ryder was sitting on the easy chair across from her, an oil lamp beside him on an ancient table, his hands folded across his flat belly and an odd smile on his face.

She started a bit. "Sorry. I guess I dozed."

"I was enjoying watching you sleep. It was soothing, so don't worry about it. Sleep whenever you need to." He waved his hand around. "Everything here is old and rickety," he remarked. "So what exactly is the story of the place? You said your husband inherited it?"

She nodded. "From his parents. Well, his dad, actually. They were older when they had him, a very late baby. I guess over the last decade or so of their lives they couldn't keep up with a lot of things. And it never occurred to Jeff to come out here and help them. He hated it out here."

"He hated it but he moved here?"

"It was free."

He nodded thoughtfully. "Okay. So the neglect is benign and he never tried to fix any of it."

"Not a thing. As long as it worked at all, it was okay."

"But his parents must have cared. I mean, there's the generator, for one thing. A good generator. And the storm shelter. If tornadoes are so rare, why did they have one?"

"Jeff said it used to be a root cellar. Some years ago there was a tornado and his dad decided to convert it."

"So he inherited the house but no money?"

Marti felt her heart stutter. "I don't know," she said finally. "But if he did…" She hesitated. "That does seem odd, doesn't it? They must have been living on something."

"Social Security might have been enough if they owned the place free and clear."

"True," she agreed. But when she thought about it, and thought of some other things, she wasn't so sure. "Water under the bridge," she said finally, deciding that trying to think about what Jeff might have concealed from her would only upset her.

"Good attitude," he agreed. "I doubt there could have been a lot of money anyway. Given the shape of the barn roof and other things. Or maybe they just didn't care, knowing Jeff never wanted to come back."

"I don't know."

"Of course you don't. Sorry I brought it up. I'm just looking at things like this table here and thinking what I could do with a little wood glue and maybe some dowels. How much I could restore. My mind runs that way," he added almost apologetically.

"That's okay."

He flashed a grin. "So do I have permission to putter freely?"

She waved a hand. "Help yourself. There's not much I can do about it right now."

"Thanks. Oh, by the way, I moved the food from the ice chest into the fridge. It's cold enough now."

Little acts of caring. They seemed so huge to her right now that she felt her throat tighten. "Thanks," she managed, hearing the thickening of her own voice.

He astonished her by rising and coming to perch on the edge of her hassock. Reaching out, he took one of her hands and rubbed it gently. "You've been through a rough time," he said.

"So have you," she pointed out.

"True. But just let me do what I do best and we'll both have less to worry about."

But what did he do best? she wondered. Was he replacing Brandy with her? Taking care of another woman to ease his heart about the one he hadn't been able to do enough for?

Maybe. She tried to tell herself it didn't matter, that she needed the help and he needed to give it. But truthfully, somewhere deep inside, she didn't want to be some other woman's replacement.

Just once in her life she wanted to feel good enough in and of herself. She wondered if she ever would.

* * *

Ryder sat there holding her hand, watching emotions flicker across her face, unreadable but suggesting some kind of sorrow. Well, yeah, he thought. This woman had her own bucketload of sorrows. He hoped he wasn't adding to them.

She couldn't possibly imagine how good it felt to him to have his efforts appreciated, even little ones like moving stuff from an ice chest to a refrigerator. For years now, most of that had zipped right past Brandy's awareness, she had been so lost in her own pain.

He was itching to fix the wobbly table but knew he couldn't do a decent job in the dim light and without some glue and dowels. At least it was stable enough to hold the oil lamp, but he found himself wondering about other places in the house. Oil lamps could be dangerous.

"Maybe we should use flashlights upstairs," he said, squeezing her hand before releasing it. "If other things are as wobbly as that table over there, the lamps are dangerous."

"I wouldn't want to carry one upstairs anyway. I wouldn't risk it, those stairs are so steep. One misstep could be ugly."

He nodded agreement. "It sure could. I watched you come down them earlier, and frankly it worried me."

"I've learned to be careful."

He was sure she had. After all, she'd grown into her current state and it was obvious to him already that she very much wanted this baby.

"I hope I get to meet Linda Marie," he said before he thought it through. He watched emotions race across her face faster than he could read and wondered if he'd said the wrong thing. But he left it alone because it was true: he wanted to meet this baby someday.

She smiled finally. "I think you already met her."

"True. And she kicked me. Maybe she doesn't want to meet me."

At that she laughed, and he felt himself respond to that beautiful sound. He wondered at himself, wondered if that was because Brandy had so infrequently laughed that the sound of a woman's laughter struck him as beautiful and rare, or if it was the sound of this woman's laughter that touched him so.

"You have a beautiful laugh," he said honestly. "Does my heart good to hear it."

He wasn't sure in the dim lighting from the oil lamps, but he thought her cheeks reddened. She looked down, pressing her hands to her bulging tummy. "I haven't laughed enough in a long time. I think it's good for her to hear it, too."

"Well, let's work on keeping it up," he suggested. The thing was, that laugh did more than tug at some of his heartstrings. It also wakened desires he hadn't felt in a long time simply because Brandy hadn't been interested in sex. Of course she hadn't, being so depressed. He understood and felt a flicker of guilt that such thoughts should even cross his mind.

It made him feel disloyal to Brandy, yet Brandy was gone and he had no reason to feel disloyal any longer. In addition, he wondered if there was something wrong with him, being attracted to a pregnant woman. Then he wondered why that should be wrong.

Damn, he was messed up, questioning his every feeling in terms of right and wrong. But Brandy had taught him that, he realized. Every thought, every feeling, had to be measured against how they would make Brandy feel, yet worrying constantly about Brandy in that way in the end hadn't helped her one bit. There were times when he'd been absolutely certain that nothing he said or did could begin to penetrate that wall of depression.

So maybe he should stop weighing everything with some invisible scale and just let his feelings flow. They couldn't hurt Brandy anymore, and as long as he didn't do something stupid, they wouldn't hurt anyone else.

He realized he was staring at Marti's belly. He dragged his gaze upward and saw that she had noticed. Something in her expression suggested that it worried her.

"Don't know if anybody's told you," he said frankly, "but pregnancy sure looks good on a woman."

Her hand fluttered to her cheek and her eyes widened. Okay, that had been too much, he supposed. He'd barely met the woman.

But she surprised him. "I haven't been feeling very pretty," she admitted, her voice muted. "I've been feeling ugly and fat."

"There's nothing fat about a baby bump," he pointed out. "It's natural, and a woman shouldn't feel ugly when she's doing something so important to the survival of the species."

Her eyes widened again and another laugh slipped from her. "If your name wasn't Kelstrom, I'd wonder if you'd kissed the Blarney stone."

He laughed, too. "Sorry, no blarney, just fact. Brandy never wanted kids. In all honesty, that was probably for the best. I don't think she could have handled the added stress."

Her smile faded. "What about you?"

"I wanted a family, back when. Then I realized it wouldn't be good for her." He shrugged.

She seized his hand, taking him by surprise yet again, and pressed it to her firm belly. "See? Linda Marie liked what you just said. And honestly, Ryder, has it occurred to you that you might be just a little too self-sacrificing?"

Him? Self-sacrificing? The idea made him uncomfortable. "Nah," he said quickly. "You just do what you have to do."

Her smile was soft. "Maybe that's what makes you special."

"If we're going in that direction, maybe I could say the same about you."

Their eyes met and locked, and for Ryder there was no mistaking the sizzle of sexual electricity that snapped between them. No mistaking the darkening of her eyes or the way her breath suddenly quickened.

Linda Marie decided to get into the act, too, kicking hard at his hand. Part of him thought it might be smart to yank his hand back to safety, but another part of him didn't want to lose the moment of magical contact.

It was almost magical, lifting him out of the lonely place he'd lived in for so long, to a place where hopes and dreams weren't lost in a sea of loss, medicines and pain.

Oh, damn, he'd better watch his step.

But the warning went unheeded as they continued to sit on, his hand pressed to her belly, her hand covering his, their eyes locked in astonishment as if they had both either wakened from sleep or had fallen into a dream.

He wanted the moment never to end.

Marti thought she could fall right into Ryder's steady gaze. She could feel the zap of sexual electricity between them, so surprising in her life now. Hell, surprising after years of feeling as if that part of her might have died.

She liked it, didn't want to let go of it, even though she knew it could amount to nothing. He was a man on a mission and would be gone in a few days. But not even that thought could quell the hunger.

God, she needed to feel desirable, needed to feel pretty and attractive. Needed to feel as if she were more than a chef and maid and something to be kicked around.

That gulf in her life had been bigger than she had honestly realized until this man had showed up and proved that Jeff wasn't the epitome of the male gender.

A man could be helpful and caring. A man could find her beautiful. A man could want her.

God, it was a heady feeling. And although she felt a flutter of fear about it, that flutter couldn't suppress years of repressed longings.

How was it possible that after little more than a day, Ryder could remind her of all the hopes and dreams that had been sacrificed on the altar of Jeff's problems? How could Ryder, with just a few words, looks and touches, awaken a woman she thought long dead, the younger Marti who had cherished what had eventually seemed like unrealistic dreams about marriage, husbands and families?

That younger self was stirring now, and trying to push her to places that she had long since learned could be dangerous.

Not good. The warning sounded loud in her mind. Such feelings couldn't be real, certainly not after such a short time.

She closed her eyes, shutting him out, and finally

made herself stir. "I'm tired," she murmured. "It's bedtime for me."

He immediately moved to help her up from her chair and get her a flashlight. She said good-night then headed for the stairs, feeling his gaze on her back every step of the way.

She was running, she realized. Running from hopes and dreams that scared her because they were so fragile.

But she kept right on climbing.

Chapter 5

His third morning at Marti's, Ryder found the chainsaw, oiled and gassed it, then headed out to turn her splintered trees into firewood. It would have plenty of time to age before winter, and he hadn't failed to note the woodstove in a corner of her living room. He wondered if it could heat the whole house, then realized he'd never find out. Hell, she probably doesn't even know, given the things she'd said about her husband.

It was still early, the day bright and clear and clinging to the last of the night's chill. Marti was up and about, so he wasn't worried about disturbing her as he yanked the cord and started the saw.

The felled trees still astonished him. He understood the tensile strength of wood to his very bones, but he was looking at some big old cottonwoods that had simply shattered under the force of that storm.

Looking at them, he could only be amazed that Marti's house had taken no more damage than it had.

Tornadoes created odd damage patterns, he'd heard, but he hadn't imagined anything this odd. Looking out across the fields, he was still shocked by that sharply cut path of destruction. When he compared it to the randomness of the destruction right around her house, it was enough to boggle the mind.

He glanced up at the roof and wondered how much longer it would be before they could get to town. He was itching like mad to patch the damn thing before another rain came through.

He cut the first tree into lengths that would fit in the firebox of her stove but left them where they were. Once he had all the trees cut up, he would have to split and stack the wood.

He paused, realizing he'd just undertaken a job that could tie him up for a week or more. Inevitably that dragged his thoughts back to Ben who had been becoming increasingly impatient for his arrival in Fresno. The questions about exactly where he was had been growing, even though most of the time his answer had been "somewhere between" a couple of cities. He'd never been all that interested in pinpointing his location because it didn't seem important. It was enough that he was heading for Fresno. And now Ben couldn't even reach him because he had no cell phone signal at Marti's.

But maybe he'd better tell Ben he was going to be late. He couldn't leave Marti with this mess only half fixed, and Ben had already been waiting for weeks. He'd understand.

He was about to start on another tree when he heard the sound of an approaching engine. Letting go of the starter rope, he turned to see Micah pulling up in his official vehicle.

"I hope you have some good news," he called out.

"Actually I do." Micah strode across the yard to join him. "That's more wood than Marti should need for the winter. Maybe she can sell some of it."

"Let's see how it stacks up. I have no idea what it takes to heat this place. Maybe you can tell me what she can safely sell when I know how many cords I have."

Micah nodded. "Well, the good news is you can get to town. Phones and electricity are back on in Conard City, but it's going to take longer to get it out here."

"Then I'd better get going if I want to get roofing supplies and more gas." He set the saw down.

Micah nodded again. "Early is better. I did get the lumberyard to put a hold on roofing stuff for you. I don't know how long they'll sit on it, though. Lots of folks in need, but talking about a widow lady with no one to help her…well…" Micah smiled faintly. "I think I had them put away enough."

"Thanks." Ryder was impressed. And he was beginning to like the sense of community around here. He brushed his hands on his jeans. "I should find out if Marti wants to come along."

"Never knew a lady who didn't like to get to town once in a while," Micah opined. "You're a contractor, right? So you know how to do all of this?"

"Yeah."

"Then when you get done here, there's probably a ton of folks around who could use your help. Give it a thought, will you?"

Micah touched the brim of his hat and headed back to his car. Ryder stood a moment, surprise holding him still. Help others after he finished here? Ben flitted across his mind again, a promise he needed to keep.

But if others needed help, was he just going to walk away?

Not likely, he realized. Not likely at all.

Marti looked out the window in time to see Micah driving away and ran out onto the porch. Ryder rounded the corner just as she got outside.

"Damn," she said. "I wanted to send his wife's pot back with him."

"We can do that soon. The roads are clear. Get on your town duds, lady. We're going shopping for roofing materials and whatever else you need."

He stepped up onto the porch beside her, and she smelled the musky scent of man and the pleasant smell of sawdust and fresh-cut wood around him on the clear, crisp air.

He not only smelled good, but he looked good, too, in his work boots, flannel shirt and jeans. Good enough to eat. Her cheeks heated and she turned quickly away. "It'll take me a few minutes," she said, hoping her voice sounded normal. "I don't dress as fast as I used to."

"Take all the time you need."

But she didn't want to take her time. She wanted to hurry. Going to town would be pleasant, and going to town with Ryder even better. Unfortunately, much as she wanted to hurry, she found herself stymied by what to wear. She wanted to look pretty, something she didn't usually worry about, but when she looked in her closet she saw the same three maternity outfits that had been there from the time she'd purchased them. Other than that, all she had were a couple of pairs of jeans with a stretch panel and a few baggy old sweatshirts.

That had been enough when she was alone, but things had changed. Dolling up had suddenly become important.

Sheesh. She told herself not to be silly. They were just going to a lumberyard. But her purchases had been practical ones, designed for maximum wear at minimum price. Because she would only wear them for a few months, she hadn't wasted money on something just because it was pretty.

Finally she scolded herself into not overdoing it and settled on her maternity jeans and one of the nicer tops. Nothing extravagant, but better than that raggedy old sweatshirt.

When she came downstairs, Ryder was waiting, and his gaze was appreciative.

"I like that top," he remarked.

She looked down at the plain navy-blue jersey and wondered if he'd lost his mind. Then she glanced at him again and a pleasant shiver of delight ran through her as it occurred to her he was remarking on what he saw in the top, not the top itself. Could that be possible?

No, of course not, she told herself firmly. He was just being polite.

But that didn't take any of the pleasure away for her. She was going to town with Ryder and it seemed like a great adventure, however boring the purpose.

"I need to call my brother-in-law when we get to town," he remarked as they headed down the road. She'd given him the keys so he could drive and was glad she had. She felt safer for the baby without the steering wheel right against her tummy, even though the seat belt might be as bad. But at least she could arrange it so it was down lower.

"You don't want to keep him waiting," she answered, trying to be decent about it even if she hated the thought of him leaving.

"He can wait. He's waited this long. But I do need to let him know I'm going to be late."

The drive into town amazed her. Alongside the road, where she could look out across rolling fields, she could see the huge tornado's path of destruction. It went on for miles and the only mercy she could see was that few houses had been in its path.

When they reached the edge of town, what she saw disturbed her even more. Although the damage hadn't been total, there was no missing the number of downed trees, the debris that homeowners had heaped at the curb, or the fact that an awful lot of people were on their roofs with shingles. Not as bad as it might have been, nowhere near as bad, but still shocking.

"This is a miss?" she finally said.

"I was wondering the same thing. It looks bad enough. Imagine if that thing had hit head-on."

She didn't want to imagine it. Conard City would have vanished from the map. As if he sensed her reaction, he reached out and clasped her hand.

"Take it easy," he said. "Believe me, folks will come back from this relatively soon. They'll be fine."

At the lumberyard, he gave his name, and to Marti's surprise an order was pulled and the employees began loading the truck.

"How did you manage this?" she asked Ryder.

"Thank Micah. He asked them to set aside what he

figured I'd need for the repair. I do want to get a few other things, though. Do you mind walking around?"

Of course she didn't mind. It felt good to be out of the house and free to look beyond her narrow walls. Before long, Ryder had a cart full of things like a tool belt, a nail gun and nails, wood glue, dowels... She didn't even know what all the stuff was, but apparently he did.

Even more amazing was that he didn't even wince when he handed over his credit card.

"That's an awful lot you just spent," she said in a subdued voice. "Ryder..."

"Don't say a word. I need this job as much as you need to have it done."

He didn't explain, leaving her to sort through all the things he had told her about how working made him feel better. The working part she could understand. The expenditure would have made her sick, though.

Then he invited her to lunch at the City Diner. While they waited to be served, he took the opportunity to use the pay phone. Watching his face across the room as he spoke troubled her. He didn't look all that happy.

He returned to the table in time for Maude to slam down their sandwiches and refill their glasses, his with water, hers with milk.

"Something wrong?" Marti asked.

"Not really. Ben seemed a little put out that I might be a few weeks later than I promised, but once I told him the gist of the situation around here, he calmed down. He just wanted to know how to reach me."

"This must be as hard on him as it is on you," she offered.

"Harder," he said flatly. "He didn't see Brandy's

struggles on a day-to-day basis. I don't think he really understands the demons she had to battle."

"I'm sorry. How in the world do you think you can explain?"

"Honestly?" His face was grim. "I don't think I can explain it. I'm just going to try to get him to accept that everything humanly possible was done. Brandy was simply too sick."

She hesitated then asked, "Do you really accept it yourself? That you did everything possible?"

"Logically I do. Emotionally I'm probably always going to wonder."

She understood that. How many hours had she wasted wondering what she might have done for Jeff that she hadn't? It was a hard thing to live with, even though her emotional ties to Jeff, that thing called love, had died long before he had. Absent love, there was a deep sense of responsibility. Even loyalty. How could you not feel at least some guilt that maybe you hadn't done quite enough?

"Maybe," she said reluctantly, "you should just get to Ben's first. If you're feeling guilty, he must be feeling even more so because he wasn't there to help."

"If he's feeling guilty he hasn't said so. I know he's angry with me, and I can understand it. But no, I'm not going to leave you at the mercy of the next thunderstorm. First things first."

"But he's family. I'm just a stranger."

He lifted one brow. "Tell me, Marti, when was the last time you felt you deserved to have anyone do something for you?"

She looked quickly away, her throat tightening. Not

for a long time, if ever, she realized. Then her throat tightened even more as he clasped her hand.

"You deserve some things," he said, "just because you're a fellow human being. It's as simple as that. Some things shouldn't have to be earned or paid for in some way."

She darted a glance at him and saw he looked deadly serious. "What do you deserve?" she asked.

"A chance to fix your roof because it'll make me feel better about myself. How's that?"

That wasn't something she could argue with.

"Give in gracefully," he suggested, "or we'll be fighting over every single nail I drive, and I'm going to be driving them anyway."

That drew a laugh from her, and she finally relaxed enough to eat and actually enjoy it.

"Oh, hell," he said as they pulled out of the grocery store parking lot where he'd insisted on taking her to pick up some essential perishables and more food—which he insisted on paying for, much to her added embarrassment. She had also discovered he had a weakness for chocolate chip cookies and when she found that out, she offered to bake them for him.

But now they were headed home, a heavy load in the back of the pickup, groceries in the crew seat behind them. "What?"

"Look over there."

She turned her attention to the west and the mountains and wanted to groan when she saw the dark clouds preceded by a white squall line. "Oh, no!"

"Oh yes. We've got to hurry. I at least want to nail up

the new tarps I bought before that hits. We don't want any leaking."

"This is supposed to be a dry climate."

"Right now you couldn't prove that by me," he answered and pressed harder on the accelerator. "If the ride gets too bouncy for you, let me know."

It wasn't too bad until they hit the gravel road about two miles from her house. She tried to ignore it, but finally a growing sense of discomfort forced her to ask him to slow down.

He immediately eased up and she was able to relax a bit. He glanced her way. "This wouldn't be my choice for a place to deliver."

"Or the time. I still have two months."

"Then easy does it."

He pulled up in front of the porch when they reached the house. "Just get inside," he said. "I'll take care of everything else."

She wanted to rebel. She didn't like feeling helpless or useless, and irritation rose in her. In that instant she no longer felt cared for, she felt like a burden.

"I can make decisions for myself," she announced before she got out of the truck.

He looked at her, turning in the seat to face her squarely. He appeared surprised by her reaction, then something in his face softened. "Of course you can. Sorry, I should have phrased that as a request. Lady, I'd feel a whole helluva lot better if you were sitting inside with your feet up, and I can grab the groceries fast and get them inside. Would you oblige me?"

She glared at him, but not for long as she realized she was being a bit ridiculous. That didn't make her feel any better, but at least it calmed her ire. She slid out of the truck and went inside, trying to figure out her nutty reaction.

She guessed she was reacting to Jeff again. He had never asked her to do something, had simply tossed out orders that she didn't dare disobey lest they wind up in a really ugly fight.

Sometimes she wished she could carve her entire experience with Jeff out of her life, then realized that would mean carving out Linda Marie also, and nothing could make her want that.

Sighing, she rubbed her eyes and tried not to watch Ryder walking by with grocery bags that she knew she was perfectly capable of carrying. He was protective, maybe too protective, and she wondered if Brandy had made him that way or if he'd always been like that.

Dumb question, she told herself. As if he would even know anymore. Just like she didn't know if she'd always been weak in some ways or if Jeff had enhanced weaknesses that were already there.

Ryder didn't give her long to ask herself unanswerable questions, though. He paused in the doorway. "Would you mind putting the groceries away? I'd like to get all that stuff from the lumberyard into a dry place— assuming I can find one in that barn."

"Sure," she answered, giving him no more because she was still a little fluffed with herself and needed some more time to settle her feathers. The image eased the last of her irritation as she suddenly thought of herself as a puffed-up sparrow getting annoyed with a very large hawk.

By the time she got to the kitchen, she was even smiling inwardly. If she was going to argue with the hawk, it would make sense to choose something important to argue about, not over carrying in some dang groceries.

Through the kitchen window, she saw him drive toward the open barn door. And beyond that she saw the squall line getting nearer. *Damn,* she thought and hurried to put stuff away. *Not another one. Please not another one.*

She started a pot of coffee, then sat to wait. Only lately had she discovered how much she hated to wait. It seemed as if she were perpetually living in expectation, and not only because of her pregnancy. Something had been telling her for a while now that Linda Marie's arrival would bring about other changes than simply having a baby. A job, definitely. Maybe a big move if she could afford it eventually. Or maybe even an inclination to become a part of this community.

But everything was on hold until then. Everything. She really couldn't do anything until the baby arrived, and that was a date circled in red on a calendar, perhaps right and perhaps wrong.

She sighed and went to turn the flame down under the coffee.

She heard Ryder on the roof, heard him moving around, even heard the hammer of his new nail gun. Now that was an extravagance, she thought, but maybe not from his perspective. Not when he probably was looking at driving hundreds of nails.

She had no difficulty imagining what he looked like up there because she had watched him after the tornado. Silhouetted against the dark sky, a powerful-looking man ignoring the lightning behind him.

The image had been sexy to her then, even in her

state of horror and shock, and now, without the horror and shock it was even sexier.

Looking down, she pulled up her pants legs and saw that her ankles had swollen slightly. Not too much and to be expected after the trip to town. She decided she'd put her feet up later, after she made the cookies. It seemed like the least she could do for the man on her roof.

By the time the second batch emitted delicious aromas from the oven, Ryder entered the kitchen, tool belt still hanging from his hips, smiling. "Damn, that smells good!"

"Fresh coffee, too," she said, pointing. "Help yourself to it and the cookies."

He put half a dozen cookies on a plate and carried them over to the table with a mug of coffee. "What can I get for you?"

"I'm fine."

He put one hand on his hips, canting them in a way that reminded her just how sexy a man's narrow hips could look. "Now listen," he said, "I'm standing. It would be easy to get you coffee or anything else. Is there some reason you want to be just fine?"

She regarded him, feeling her brow crease. "Because I am fine?" He studied her in a way that made her feel as if he could see right through her. She wondered how much of that came from trying to read Brandy's mind. How often he must have tried to see beyond the surface so he could gauge the pain beneath. "Do you have a problem with someone being fine?"

His brows arched, then he pulled out a chair and sat facing her. "I guess I do," he admitted.

"Why?"

"Because every time Brandy said that it meant a brewing storm."

"God, that would be awful!" The words burst out of her. "Sorry. Not my place. But I've known people like that. When they say, 'I'm fine' they're anything but."

"With Brandy that was sure true. I learned to translate it as meaning she was anything *but* fine but she didn't want to talk about it right then. Eventually she would explode or curl up in tears. I got so I hated those words. Sorry."

"I can't imagine how rough it must have been."

"Maybe no rougher than what you went through. It was what it was, you know? I loved that woman, and it wasn't like she caused her own illness. She was blameless. You might get frustrated at times, but you can't hate someone for being sick."

No, she thought. But you could stop loving them. That caused her a twinge of guilt, but she pushed it away. Her love for Jeff had died. It hadn't been a choice—it had just happened. One morning she had awakened and felt icy inside when she saw him. She'd known with certainty that whatever she once felt for that man had vanished.

He sighed, then bit into a cookie. His face brightened immediately. "These are great!"

"I'm making six dozen, so enjoy." She summoned a smile, dragging her thoughts away from marriages past. "You're certainly going to work them off. What were you doing out there?"

"Putting up those new tarps I bought. Less likely to leak. I just hope the weather clears soon so I can get to the repairs."

And so he could leave sooner. Her heart plummeted. Then a worry popped up. "Ryder?"

"Hmm?" His mouth was full of cookie.

"How in the world are you going to get that plywood and those shingles up there? The plywood is heavy and awkward, and although I suppose you could carry one bundle of shingles on your back at a time…" She shook her head. "I just don't see how you can do it."

"That's what they make ropes for. Trust me—I can do it."

"But won't the plywood swing around?"

"The ladder," he reminded her. "I pull it up flat against the ladder. As long as the wind cooperates, it'll work."

"Like the wind ever really stops out here."

"But it's not usually very strong. Just constant. Not as bad as it was when I passed through South Dakota. The wind there makes a soda bottle sing."

"You have been wandering."

"Good chance to really see the country."

She noticed all of a sudden that the day had darkened. At once she rose and went to look out the window over the sink. "Not again," she murmured.

She realized that Ryder had come to stand beside her. "It's just a storm."

"Maybe." Never before had an ordinary thunderstorm frightened her. Up until a few days ago, she had always enjoyed them. Right now she was feeling queasy at the appearance of the sky, and dread started creeping along her nerve endings.

"Are you scared?" he asked quietly.

"Aren't you, after what just happened?"

He reached over and flipped on the battery-operated radio. Some tinny bluegrass emerged. "They don't sound worried," he said.

"Not yet." Her entire body seemed to be waking to a potential threat, and Linda Marie stirred as if she felt the uneasiness. Then her nose picked up something else. "Oh, my gosh, the cookies!"

He stepped aside to let her pull out the sheet, just in time. They already looked a tad too brown. She set it on the counter to cool for a few minutes, trying to focus on the ordinary activity, planning to put another sheet in.

"That dough will hold, won't it?" he asked.

She turned and found him only inches away. "Yeah," she said uneasily. "I can just put it in the fridge."

"Then we'll do that for now. You don't look so good."

"I'm just nervous. It's stupid, I know, but after that tornado…" She bit her lip.

"It's not stupid. Not stupid at all. But as long as they're playing bluegrass, everything's okay, right?"

"Right." She tried to say it with conviction.

"Aw, lady." He sighed, then did the most amazing thing in the world. He wrapped her in his powerful arms and drew her gently against his chest.

In an instant she forgot the storm. In an instant fear faded to be replaced by a wondrous sense of safety. Never had she imagined just how good it could feel to have strong arms around her. Not ever, because she'd never felt this way before.

He shifted her a little so that she stood sideways to him and cradled her shoulders securely in one arm while his other tucked around her thickened waist. As huge as she'd been feeling lately, he made her feel small.

With a temerity that should have shocked her but didn't, he gently rubbed her tummy. "You and Linda Marie are going to be just fine," he said quietly. "If it'll make you feel safer, I can take you to the shelter."

Safer? How could she possibly feel any safer than she did at this moment? What's more, she didn't want to give up the shelter of his arms for that dank hole in the ground. As far as she was concerned, there was no choice to be made.

She gave a little shake of her head, then heard a roll of thunder that quickened her fear again.

"It's just an ordinary old storm," he repeated as the radio confirmed his words with a new song.

What she was feeling now was nothing ordinary. She tilted her head to look up at him and found him regarding her from those silvery eyes of his. Liquid silver, she thought. Hot silver.

Heat leaped in her in response, driving every other thought out of her head. Let the storm blow outside. The only storm that mattered was the one inside her.

He must have read her response because now his eyes darkened, and his lids drooped a little.

"You're so beautiful," he whispered. "Absolutely beautiful."

The compliment should have overwhelmed her. It was not as if she'd heard that very often over the past years. Nor had pregnancy made her feel anything but ungainly and fat. But before it quite penetrated, his hand left her tummy to cradle her cheek. Then, glory of glories, he dipped his head to kiss her gently.

The world went away. She lost awareness of anything except the gentle quest of his lips against hers. The contradictorily soothing search that ignited a wildfire inside her.

She gasped with the pleasure of it, and he took it as an invitation, slipping his tongue past her lips into the warm depths of her mouth. As if he wanted to possess her. As if he already did.

Waves of passion began to pulse through her in time to the thrusts of his tongue. She wanted it to go on forever. Then she wanted it to grow. She needed more but didn't know how to ask for it.

She responded as ardently as she knew how to his kiss, raising a hand to cup his cheek the way he cupped hers, enjoying the roughness of a day's stubble, the hard line of his jaw, the way his cheek moved as his tongue mated with hers.

Enjoying the growing depth of her own need.

But just as she was about to whisper that need, just as it was about to push her to become bold, thunder cracked so loudly and so close that everything inside her seemed to freeze.

Her eyes opened wide. Ryder lifted his head and looked around. He swore.

She felt like swearing, too. The moment had been destroyed and destroyed way too early. Common sense didn't seem to want to return.

"Hell," he said, adding to the colorful curse he had started with. "Damn."

He looked like one upset and angry man. That might have frightened her because of Jeff, but somehow the silliness of the moment caught her instead and she giggled.

He looked down at her again, lifting one brow. "Okay, my timing sucks. I was outta line anyway."

She pressed a finger to his lips. "Don't say that. Please don't say that."

"Okay, I won't." He sighed, then astonished her by scooping her up into his arms and carrying her to the living room where he put her in her favorite chair and lifted her feet onto the hassock. "Look at those ankles," he remarked as her jeans pulled up a bit. "I don't know damn all about pregnancy, but aren't you supposed to take care of swelling ankles?"

"Yes," she admitted.

"Then keep your butt in your chair. I'll get you something to drink. Food, if you want. Just tell me what sounds good."

So she asked for iced coffee and sat with her hands folded over Linda Marie, trying to absorb the storm that had just passed through her, leaving her feeling almost like a different person.

A man had wanted to kiss her. An attractive man. And he'd told her she was beautiful. Now didn't that beat all?

Ryder returned five minutes later with a tall glass of iced coffee for her, a plate of cookies to put at her elbow, and another for himself.

"I put the dough in the fridge," he remarked, "and yes, I covered it. I also turned off the oven for now. So just relax. I'll be back in a second with the radio."

Unfortunately, now that her intense arousal had settled down, the storm outside seemed to demand her attention. It sounded bad and her estimation of it was being affected by the tornado from four days ago. How could it not be?

She tried to argue herself into a reasonable calm. The radio would broadcast a warning, first of all. Second, why would a tornado strike the same place twice? Not likely.

But as flashes of brilliant lightning washed out the color in the room, she wasn't so sure of her estimation of the odds.

Ryder returned with the radio, which had switched from bluegrass to Garth Brooks, and set it on top of the useless console TV. "It may sound bad out there, but it doesn't seem to be worrying anybody."

"No," she admitted. "I just wonder if I'll ever feel the same about a thunderstorm again."

"Not for a while, I expect." He sat across from her. It was only a small distance away, but it seemed significant. He was right, she thought dismally. Whatever was happening between them, it didn't promise the long term. Better not to get even minimally involved.

In fact, she should be wary and so should he. They were both just emerging from bad marriages, which probably made them too vulnerable to anything that would make them feel better. Damn, she hated logic.

"Tell me about Ben," she suggested, hoping to find safer ground and distraction. Another crack of thunder made both her and the baby jump.

"Ben?" He paused. "Seems like a great guy."

"Seems?" She caught the word and thought it significant.

"Oh, he's one of those charming guys who could probably sell ice to Eskimos, if you get my drift. Lots of charisma, always ready with a joke, cheerful, likable. He draws people like honey draws flies."

"But you don't trust that?"

He hesitated. "He loved Brandy." As if that answered everything.

"But?" she repeated. "It's practically hanging on every word."

He smiled faintly. "I guess I have a native distrust of folks who are glib and charming. The problem is me, I suppose, not him. I mean, he seems sincere, especially about Brandy. But..." He shrugged. "Sometimes I get the feeling he has a hard core, if you know what I mean."

"I know exactly what you mean. Yet you still feel you need to go talk to him."

"There are wounds here, Marti. For both of us. Maybe if we just hash it out it will help. I get the feeling he thinks I could have done more. Maybe he was right. And if he's right, then he needs to tell me because I need to know for me."

There was little she could say, knowing next to nothing about the situation. So she asked, "Didn't you say you did everything the docs told you?"

"Of course I did. Every single thing. But in the end I have to ask myself if it wasn't a failure of care, but a failure on my part. Something I didn't say, something I didn't feel, something I didn't think of."

"Those are the kinds of questions that can drive you crazy."

"No kidding. Hence the Johnny Appleseed trip across the country. Time to think. And that's why I want to see Ben. Maybe he's got some answers that aren't apparent to me."

"If Ben's already blaming you, maybe he's not the best person to ask those questions." As soon as she spoke, her own temerity surprised her. She didn't know squat about this guy's marriage, about Ben, or about what had happened.

"Maybe," he said, lifting one corner of his mouth. "And maybe what I need is a harsh critic."

"I think you're already the harshest critic you could find." Immediately she wished she could call the words back. Damn, she needed to stop offering opinions when she knew next to nothing. "Sorry. I don't know enough to have an opinion."

"It's okay. You might be right. Only time will tell."

He fell silent, and this time she kept her mouth shut. What did she know about depression or relationships or anything else? Her own marriage was a sorry lesson in how messed up things could get and how you sometimes couldn't even figure out what to do. All it had done was make her an authority on screwing up. Hardly a guideline.

Rain started to fall, blowing hard enough to rattle like ice at the windows. She jumped and tried to see out the window over her shoulder. "I hope that's not hail." Hail meant tornadoes. Where had she learned that? Was it even true?

"I'll go look."

He only went as far as the front door, but even that short distance left the room feeling empty. The sensation surprised her because she hadn't felt the house was empty even after Jeff's death. That was sad, she supposed, but she felt more concern about how Ryder's momentary disappearance affected her. She really needed to stop this before she got in any deeper.

He was gone only a minute, but his return filled the room. "It's not hail. It's just the rain hitting the glass hard."

He remained standing. "What do you want me to make for dinner?"

"I can do that."

He eyed her ankles. "I'd like you to reconsider that, if you wouldn't mind. The swelling still hasn't come down."

"I always have some late in the day. It can't stop me from doing ordinary things or I'll go nuts."

A chuckle escaped him. "I know that feeling. All right, we'll do it together when you're ready, but I'm bringing the hassock into the kitchen."

He seemed to have caretaker built into his genes. "Who takes care of you, Ryder?"

He appeared startled. Then, "Well, I seem to remember some lady saving me from a tornado, and she's been making me some pretty fine meals, not to mention cookies..."

She had to laugh, even though she knew full well he hadn't answered her core question. But maybe she already knew the answer: Ryder took care of Ryder. She had been doing the same for herself until his arrival, and she knew from personal experience how empty life could seem when you didn't have even one other person who did just a few caring things for you.

You started to feel you didn't deserve them. Hadn't he brought that problem up himself, asking her what she felt she deserved?

Ryder measured himself by taking care of others, she decided, a good metric to a point. But what had he said about people deserving care just because they were people? That it shouldn't have to be earned or paid for?

Maybe Ryder needed to be on the receiving end if she could just figure out how.

There had to be a way, something she could do to express her gratitude, some way she could make him feel as if he really mattered, too, the way he was making her feel.

Yes, she would figure out something.

* * *

Ryder wanted to go to the attic and check on the tarps. The way the wind was blowing he feared it might push some water in. But given how Marti jumped at every sound and crack of thunder, he didn't want to leave her alone.

He could understand her fear. He shared some of it himself. That had been one hell of a storm, and he figured he was probably lucky to be alive. He was also fairly certain he owed that to Marti picking him up and sharing her shelter.

He might escape the uneasiness when he hit the West Coast. Or when he went back East, but here he couldn't quite evade it, no matter how rare that kind of event was supposed to be.

It hadn't affected him as much as it had her, though. Of that he was certain. He might be a little more alert than normal as the thunderstorm rolled over them with its rage, but he wasn't jumping at every crack of thunder or pellet-spray of rain.

He wished he had some magic words to take that fright from her. He didn't want to imagine her here alone when he left in a couple of weeks, dealing with that terror all by herself. But he didn't see what he could do about that.

Inevitably, he remembered holding her and kissing her and how good it had felt. She had felt just right against him, and her mouth had been so sweet. He would have liked to have carried that a whole lot farther.

Saved by the lightning, he thought with an almost bitter amusement. He wasn't anywhere near ready to consider another relationship, and Marti struck him as the kind to deserve that, not a one-night stand. But he had to get on to Ben eventually. Then he had to sort out his own head enough so he might be good for something.

Right now he figured he wasn't useful for much except hard physical work. He hoped he would be able to help Ben, though. That brother-in-law of his was hanging out there like an important, unfinished chore. He owed Brandy's brother at least that much.

But as he thought about Ben, disquiet stirred. First, he didn't like that Ben was getting angry about how long it was taking him. Eight months had passed already. What could a couple of extra weeks matter?

He wondered, too, for the first time, if Ben might be exactly the wrong person to talk to. Marti might have had that right: if Ben was so angry with him, the conversation might only be destructive.

So what was this? A mea culpa for sins he was unaware of but sure he must have committed? Did he need someone to beat him up to feel better?

The idea that his thinking might be that far out of joint disturbed him. He'd thought of this as a mercy mission for both him and Ben. Maybe it was masochistic instead.

Thinking over his conversations with Ben during the past few weeks, that discomfort grew. Ben was angry. Of course he was angry, but he'd all but exploded earlier when Ryder had told him he was hanging around out here for a couple of weeks to help a widow lady. Then he had suddenly calmed down. What had calmed him? The information about exactly where he was? Marti's name?

Maybe it was the name as much as anything, a reassurance that Ryder wasn't just stalling. But how well did he really know Ben? After five years of marriage to Brandy, the guy was still a stranger to him in a lot of ways. Impenetrable behind all that charisma and hail-fellow-well-met surface. Had Ben ever shared a genuine feeling with him other than anger over Brandy?

If so, he couldn't remember it.

That brought him right back to thinking about what he truly hoped to achieve with this trip. Peace? He doubted he would find it. Understanding? Was he hoping that Ben might be able to relate stories from Brandy's past that would illuminate her problems? Was he hoping if they both just sat and talked it through for as long as they needed they might reach acceptance if nothing else?

Something in him had clearly needed to make this journey, but he was beginning to wonder what and why. Ben's hostility toward him had often been overt since Brandy's death, but he had thought he understood it and could help with it.

But could he? Did he really understand? Maybe nothing could ease Ben's hostility any more than Ryder could fully shed his feelings of guilt.

Crap, he was beginning to think he needed a shrink himself. His thoughts had begun to resemble a mouse scrambling for an escape hatch. But there was no escape from this mess. Not since Brandy had made it final.

Maybe that was the truth he needed to get around to accepting: there was no escape.

He yanked himself out of his own head and looked at Marti again. She was sitting quietly, hands folded over her tummy, eyes closed, listening to the storm.

He wondered if she had any idea just how sexy she was, even while pregnant. Or maybe because she was pregnant. He didn't know because he had no comparison with Marti-not-expecting. But she was sexy enough to make his pulse race merely by looking at her.

Then he wondered why he was just sitting here and doing nothing about it. She hadn't repulsed his kiss earlier—in fact, she'd told him not to apologize for it. Maybe she was as hungry as he for that kind of connection.

He'd caught her looking at him a few times with the same sexual appreciation he was feeling. Was he being a gentleman by ignoring it or an idiot? Very possibly an idiot. One thing was for sure—he knew he had failed his five-year mind-reading course with Brandy.

Marti heard Ryder stir and opened her eyes in time to see him closing the distance between them. Her heart tripped then sped up as she caught the intensity in his gaze.

He perched on the arm of her chair, touched her cheek and hair, then started lowering his mouth toward hers.

"Tell me to drop dead if you don't want this."

The notion never even crossed her mind. What did cross her mind was that she wanted this to be more than a kiss.

He lowered his head until their lips touched, and she tilted her face up to him like a flower seeking the sun. At first his mouth nestled gently against hers, a gentleness that made her heart ache with longing before it struck the tinder of her body.

Again and again he lowered his head, just barely tasting, his mouth soft and questioning, until her lips started to feel as sensitive as the most secret places of her body. Little streams of pleasure began to trickle from them to the rest of her body, teaching her a new lesson in passion: patience and tenderness.

A door to a whole new world began to open to her, a

world where desire didn't have to be hasty, demanding and impatient. A world where it was a tender journey of discovery rather than a destination to be reached as quickly as possible. She loved it.

When at last his tongue slipped past her sweetly sensitive lips into the warm interior of her mouth, she welcomed and savored it, letting it go on as long as he wanted. She encouraged him only with little murmurs of pleasure and a hand on the arm on which he propped himself.

He even paused to smile at her and look deeply into her eyes, adding an intimate awareness she'd never experienced before. He knew who he was kissing, unlike Jeff who had seemed not to care who he was with as long as he got what he wanted.

She returned Ryder's smile then sighed as he began to kiss her again. He cradled her cheek, rubbing his thumb slowly over it, then left her mouth to begin sprinkling butterfly kisses on her cheeks and throat.

He made her feel worshipped.

When at long last his hand trailed lower and began to lightly caress her breast, she discovered a new sensitivity that she had never experienced before. It must have grown with her pregnancy because never before had the lightest touch of a man's hand catapulted her so far so fast.

Now she needed and wanted with an unfamiliar strength, but he still caressed her lightly. No hard squeezing, no pinching, no demanding massage of tender flesh. Just a light, almost teasing touch.

Then he did something that made her breath catch in her throat. He returned to kissing her, plunging his tongue deeply, but he dropped his hand from her breast to her belly, rubbing it gently over the entire mound of her pregnancy, cherishing her in a way she could scarcely believe. Cherishing Linda Marie, as well.

By the time he stopped and lifted his head to gaze again into her eyes, she was certain that Ryder was a man she could trust with her body. Wherever he chose to take her. That he didn't find her pregnancy an obstruction, but instead counted it an important part of her.

From hazy eyes she looked up at him and saw him smile.

"I liked that," he murmured.

"Me, too," she managed to whisper.

He swept her short, curly hair back from her face, rained a few more kisses on her, gave her one last caress, then returned to his seat.

She wished he hadn't stopped, but she understood. In the deepest reaches of her being she understood. This man didn't want to move too fast or risk taking advantage of her.

In that moment, even though she knew she would lose it, she gave a tiny piece of her heart to Ryder Kelstrom.

Chapter 6

Ben Hansen became an even angrier man when he tried to make travel arrangements to get to Ryder in Conard City, Wyoming. He didn't like to be stymied when he wanted something, but he grew purely furious when he found out how difficult it was going to be to get there.

Count on Ryder to disappear to a place at the ends of the earth and decide to hang out. Oh, the place had an airport, but given the way airlines had established major hubs and then contracted with puddle-jumper airlines, he would have to go around his butt to get to his elbow.

This was the twenty-first century, he thought, trying not to bash a hand on his computer as he looked at the number of flights and the schedules. It shouldn't be this hard to get anywhere.

But it was. No matter where he looked, he found

that he'd have to take a minimum of three flights, with hours of layovers.

Who the hell would have thought that you had to fly to Minneapolis or Chicago to get to a place in between there and here?

Oh, there were other options, but they just got uglier. If he wanted to skip the flying halfway across the country so he didn't have to fly back half the distance, his other option, although more direct, meant he'd be stopping and often changing planes in every rube airport in the west.

He ground his teeth and tried to make up his mind. At this point it might make more sense to drive, but he didn't want to leave that kind of record behind him. Ryder had to die for what he'd done to Brandy, but damn, Ben wasn't going to leave a DayGlo trail behind.

His head snapped up suddenly as he realized something. Flying or driving his own car was out. Either way he could be traced.

So, he'd rent a car, tell the rental people he was driving to Vegas, and he wouldn't mention that he was going to take as circuitous a route as any airline.

He began to feel better. Rent the car, get plenty of cash so he wouldn't leave a trail of credit card slips behind him, detour to this damn Conard City, take care of business and show up maybe a day or so late in Vegas. Who would know? Especially if he dropped off the car there and said he didn't need it until he was ready to go back to Fresno.

The more he thought about it, the more he liked it. Where that car went, as long as he got one without GPS and he didn't carry his cell phone, wouldn't be traceable. Not at all.

And all the world would know was that while Ryder was killed, Ben had been in Vegas.

He'd have to make a hotel reservation. Okay, he'd have to go to Vegas first, check into a hotel for cover, then take a trip to Wyoming. That would work.

The more he thought about it, the more his anger eased. Ryder was going to get his comeuppance at last.

So maybe it was a damn good thing Ryder had stopped to help the widow lady. Yes, the more he thought about it, the better he liked it. It was just the opportunity he needed.

No ties, no links, no reason for anyone to suspect Ben.

It was an excellent plan.

The next morning, Ryder was just getting ready to haul roofing materials up the ladder when a pickup he hadn't seen before pulled up in front of Marti's house. The guy who climbed out appeared to be about sixty, with gold hair and a neat beard gone almost gray, but fit. From the other side of the truck, a boy in his late teens emerged.

Ryder slid down the ladder and walked over.

"Howdy," the man said. "I'm Ransom Laird, and this is my son Marcus. Micah Parish said you might need some help this morning."

Ryder immediately shook their hands. "Ryder Kelstrom. You get through the storm okay?"

"Yeah. I have a ranch about fifteen miles northwest of here and we took only a little wind damage. Let me pay my respects to Mrs. Chastain and then we'll get on with helping you."

"Thanks, I really appreciate it."

So, he thought as he followed the two men to the front door, the neighborliness around here existed. The local tom-tom had sent out the message the widow lady needed help. It tickled him, especially when Marti had been frank about knowing no one.

For all she had chosen to be isolated before, Marti welcomed her neighbors warmly, invited them in and offered to make coffee.

"Coffee after we get the heavy stuff on the roof," Ransom said. "The way the weather's been, we might not have all the time in the world."

Extra hands made the job easier by far. It proved relatively easy to pull away the tarps, cast them to the ground, and replace them with plywood sheathing. An extra nail gun would have helped, but Marcus, who looked like a young clone of his father, proved to be handy with a hammer.

Ryder couldn't have asked for much better than a morning under a warm sun working on a roof with a couple of nice guys. The heavy labor worked its usual magic, driving all the nightmares of his past into the background. Maybe, he thought, once he'd taken care of Ben he'd get back into construction but not as a general contractor. No, he liked the actual hands-on, hard work too much. He also enjoyed the camaraderie, and cabinet making wouldn't give him that.

About the time they had finished laying the tar paper over the plywood, it was lunchtime and the sky to the west was darkening again.

Ransom plopped down on an undamaged portion of the roof and stared at the sky. "We're not going to have time to get the shingles up today. Maybe we should tarp it over."

Ryder, standing beside him on the sloping roof, eyed the storm, too. "Is it going to do this every day?"

Ransom shrugged. "Danged if I know. This isn't normal weather. We're mostly in the rain shadow of the mountains. But then, weather hasn't really been normal for a few years. It used to be pretty arid around here. It makes a lot of good grazing for my sheep, but it doesn't make it easy to do anything else."

Ransom cocked his head, looking up at Ryder. "We can try to get as much done as possible. I'm not opposed. It's just that these storms have been moving in fast."

"I'd rather not have to nail up tarps over new shingles," Ryder said. "Seems crazy to put holes in a new roof. And we still haven't put up all the flashing."

At that moment, Marti's voice reached them from below. "Lunch is ready!"

That seemed to settle the issue. Marcus climbed down to recover the tarps, and they spent about fifteen minutes nailing them back in place before they climbed down.

"We can come back in the morning and help you finish up," Ransom assured him. "Marcus won't have any school for a week or two, and keeping a kid his age busy is always wise."

Marcus rolled his eyes. "Dad!"

"Not enough syllables in that protest," Ransom said with a wink. "You're supposed to drag it out."

"Why no school?" Ryder asked as they headed inside.

"Roof and window damage. Lots of folks are pitching in, but they've got their own problems to deal with."

"Maybe I can help when I get this done."

"We'd appreciate it," Ransom said. "Well, I will. I'm not so sure about Marcus."

That earned him another eye roll and the two older men were laughing as they went inside.

Ryder stepped into the kitchen and wondered if Marti had spent all morning cooking. Far from the sandwiches he would have expected, she'd turned out a full chicken dinner and a pie was cooling on the counter. Plenty of food and plenty of coffee and soon plenty of conversation.

Of course, most of the subjects were alien to him, and probably to Marti as well, but she seemed to enjoy hearing about the ups and downs of raising sheep, a subject on which even Marcus grew voluble.

Then there was the family stuff: Ransom's wife, Mandy, who was a published novelist, and three kids. By the time they got to the pie, Ryder had even mentioned Brandy and that he was a widower, more than he'd expected to say from the outset but sufficient to explain a few things.

By the time they helped Marti clear up, Ransom had promised that Mandy would drop by soon and it seemed a friendship had begun to form.

Good. The more people she knew, the better he'd feel about moving on. But he was also getting a sense of how easy it would be to sink into the rhythms of this place: hard work, friendship, a kind of easiness among people he wasn't really used to.

It was, he thought with surprise, almost as seductive as Marti herself. And that was saying something.

After lunch, the looming storm moved in and it was far worse than the one the day before. This one literally shook the walls, and although there were no weather warnings other than of wind and flash floods near some creeks, it didn't make either of them relax.

"God," Marti said finally, "I don't know if I can stand this!"

"We can go to the shelter," Ryder offered.

But she shook her head at him. While terror clawed at her, a stubborn streak she'd always had reared up. "I've got to learn to stand it," she said, her fists clenched. "There will always be thunderstorms. I can't have a nervous breakdown over every one. Even if I could stand it, it wouldn't be good for Linda Marie."

She watched Ryder pull back to that place inside himself, a place he went every now and then that left her feeling alone even when he was right there. She could only wonder what he was thinking about; she didn't ask. Something about those occasional withdrawals suggested he needed to be left alone with his thoughts.

Probably thinking about Brandy, she thought. A woman with a serious emotional disease. God, maybe she was reminding him of his wife with this irrational behavior. She didn't want to do that, but she didn't know how she could stop. It was hard enough to sit in this damn chair with her swollen ankles elevated and not curl up into a tight ball.

One storm. Now a phobia. Sheesh, she needed to get past this.

The walls and windows rattled again, and she wondered if the whole place was going to collapse on them. It was old and she had absolutely no idea how well it had been maintained. It certainly hadn't been maintained since Jeff had inherited it.

She squeezed her eyes shut and forced herself to breathe deeply and slowly. It was just a storm. Just an ordinary thunderstorm. Not a killer, unless she did something stupid. Wind and rain and lightning. It happened dozens of times a year.

Her eyes snapped open as she felt her ballet slippers being tugged off her feet. She watched in astonishment as Ryder began to massage her toes gently.

"Ryder?"

"You talk to the doctor about this swelling?"

"I'm okay. It's normal."

"Guess that's what you get for spending all morning cooking a gourmet meal for the help." He flashed a smile that took any possible sting out of the words.

The storm was still howling, but it seemed to recede as he worked gently on her feet, from her toes to just above her ankles, as if to encourage the swelling to move out.

Before long, she wanted to purr. It was such a change in mood that it amazed her. But then she'd never had a foot massage before, nor dreamed that one could feel so good.

Over and over his hands continued their gentle work, and the longer he went at it, the more relaxed she felt.

"You have pretty feet," he remarked.

"They look like overstuffed sausages," she retorted.

He laughed. "Overstuffed or not, they're pretty, like everything else about you." He grasped her heel and flexed her toes upward at the same time, and she felt a deep tension let go. "Why does this happen?"

"My doc says it's the change in body chemistry, along with increasing pressure from the baby. Nothing to worry about unless I start seeing it in my face, or my hands swell too much."

"I'm glad it's nothing to worry about but it doesn't look comfortable."

"I usually don't feel it at all."

"I suppose that's good." His hands began kneading a little harder but not enough to hurt. Odd how it seemed to be taking the tension out of her entire body.

She let her head fall back and closed her eyes as his magical hands sent waves of relaxation throughout her entire body.

The storm seemed to be receding, though whether it really was or she was just ignoring it better she didn't know. All she knew was that the tension was seeping away and she was glad to let it go.

"You can do that anytime you want," she told him.

He chuckled quietly. "I may take you up on it. I'm enjoying it."

"Every time it storms."

"If that's what you want."

Of course, he wouldn't be here every time it stormed. She tried to remember that, but another sensation began to replace the gooey relaxation that had cascaded through her. Now that she wasn't worrying about the storm, wasn't filled with irrational fear, she noticed something else.

How good his touch felt. How warm his hands were. A sweeter tension began to fill her, rising from the hands that worked gently on her feet and ankles, following a whole new course to her very center. A whole new world, she thought again, he was showing her a whole new world.

She tried not to stir as he continued the massage, but the sensations spreading up her legs to her center made that very difficult. She had forgotten how good that particular deep throbbing could feel. Had forgotten it was possible to be so needy and hungry for a man's touch.

The doors Ryder had started opening were swinging wide now, flooding her with sensations, making her realize how paltry and limited her previous experience had been.

It was like a bad joke, she thought hazily. The man she had married had made her wonder what the big deal about sex was. The man who was going to leave her in a few short days was teaching her just how great it was with the gentlest, most unobjectionable touches.

"Ryder?" she asked, knowing she might be getting into deep trouble.

"Hmm?"

"Have you ever had great sex?"

His hands froze for a second, then resumed massaging. "Yeah. A very long time ago. At least I remember it as being great."

"I never have. I thought it was one big disappointment and couldn't understand why it was such a huge deal."

Again his hands froze. Then he whispered, "Oh, lady, you just handed me a grenade."

She opened her eyes to half mast. "Grenade? What do you mean?"

"I've been wanting you since I laid eyes on you. Now you've all but asked me. Tell me you don't mean it."

"Why?"

"You know all the reasons. You're pregnant. I'll be leaving eventually to go see Ben, I'm an emotional train wreck… Why in God's name would you want to get mixed up with me even temporarily?"

She barely hesitated. "Because I want to know."

He released her ankles. "Better to learn that from a guy better than me."

At least he didn't go away. But he'd certainly killed the desire and replaced it with anger. "Just what is wrong with you?" she demanded. "You're a really nice guy, you know. And what happened with Brandy wasn't your fault. She was sick."

"If I'm not sure I didn't screw it up somehow, how can you be? You hardly know me."

"I know what I've seen since you got here. My own husband didn't take half as good care of me. In fact, he didn't much give a damn. You—well there's hardly been an instant when you haven't been trying to take care of me. That's tells me a lot. You even worry about my swollen ankles. So excuse me if I seriously doubt that you failed Brandy in any way. She was just too sick to know what a good man she had!"

Oh, that had done it. He was up like a shot, and vanished out into the storm, slamming the door behind him.

What the hell had gotten into her? She wondered this as a tear began to roll down her cheek. What had she been thinking? Who was she to talk about anyone's relationships?

Maybe it was some kind of weird hormone attack. Or maybe she was reacting to all the years when she had kept her mouth shut. Years when she had put up and shut up.

A stranger was comparatively easy pickings, wasn't he?

She brought her fist to her mouth and tried to quell the tears, but they wouldn't stop. She tried to tell herself pregnant women were just weepy.

But there was no escaping the pain in her heart.

* * *

Ryder stormed out to the barn where he watched rain drizzle through a roof he itched to repair. He made sure the tarp adequately protected the stuff in the bed of the pickup, then wandered around looking for something, anything to do.

But the rain had been heavy enough to drench him on his pilgrimage to this male bastion, and soon he noticed he was sopping, that he was starting to shiver and that he was a damn fool.

All the woman had done was try to say something nice to him. To tell him she thought he was a good man and that maybe logic was right when it said that the fault had lain with Brandy's illness. Crap, Brandy and her doctors had been telling him that for a long time. He'd been arguing with himself about that forever.

Finally he found an old, moldy bale of hay and just sat on it, ignoring his shivering. Okay, what if the docs were right? What if it was all her illness? Why was he fighting that possibility so hard?

Because he hated not being in control.

Because he hated being helpless.

And Brandy had made him feel both of those things acutely.

He'd built a small business empire from the ground up, starting with framing. By the time he had begun his own contracting business, there wasn't a thing he didn't know about the building trade, not a thing he couldn't do with his own hands if necessary.

And then he'd discovered that by moving up he'd lost some control. He couldn't be everywhere at once. He couldn't watch every single worker. He'd had to run on a certain amount of trust, and it had left him always uneasy.

That was why he'd never been really happy with having his own business and why he was thinking about returning to cabinetry. Because he would control every single detail.

But he couldn't control Brandy. He couldn't control her illness no matter how many pills or how many doctors. He couldn't help her much either, which made him feel useless. And then she'd taken the last bit of control away by killing herself.

His problem, he realized as he sat there shaking ever more violently, was that he couldn't deal with the fact that in life you actually had very little control over most things.

Bad things happened no matter how hard you tried to prevent them. All the best laid plans, all the buffers, all the struggles and sometimes life was just going to get the better of you.

He knew Ben blamed him. And that was exactly the reason he was going to visit him: so someone could lay the blame squarely on him where he felt it belonged, unlike the doctors who kept telling him he'd done everything he could.

He didn't want forgiveness, he wanted blame. And why? Because he wasn't God?

He swore, the words lost in the pounding of the rain and a rumble of thunder.

Damn, he'd left Marti all alone in there when she was terrified of this storm. What the hell was wrong with him? Maybe he hadn't failed Brandy, but he was going to prove his worthlessness anyway by leaving that woman alone to deal with her terror?

Furious at himself, he headed back for the house, the rain beating on him almost as hard as if it were hail.

When he stepped inside, he knew he'd made a huge mistake. The radio was blasting the emergency warning.

Marti had dropped her feet to the floor and was sitting hunched over, trembling from the instant she heard the unmistakable beeping. Not another tornado, please.

Flood warnings. Wind warnings, lightning warnings, but no tornadoes even mentioned. She was trying to un-cramp her hands and force herself to lean back when she heard Ryder come through the door.

He looked like a wildman. Water was dripping from him like a private downpour, and a puddle began to rapidly form around his booted feet.

"How bad is it?" he demanded.

She waved to the radio as the electronic voice began its repetition of current warnings.

"That's not so bad," he said as the beeping returned.

"You're soaked," she said, hoping she sounded more relaxed than she felt. "Go change. If only we had some hot water…"

"Back in a sec," he said, and she listened to the heavy thuds as he ran up the stairs. It took more than a second, of course, because not even a quick-change artist could doff clingy drenched clothes fast.

With effort, she made herself lean back and put her feet up again. Then she loosened her hands and laid them on the arms of her chair, hoping Ryder couldn't see how tightly she was clinging to them.

Just a storm, she repeated like a mantra. Just a stu-pid storm, not a catastrophe. She wondered how it was possible for one incident to give her such an enduring fear. It had to pass. It had to.

At long last she heard Ryder come hurrying down the stairs, his tread lighter now that he had ditched his work boots. He appeared wearing dry jeans and a flannel shirt, and his hair looked a little wild from toweling.

"You okay?" was the first thing he asked.

"Better," she lied. Or maybe it wasn't a lie because just seeing him made her feel better. No longer was she alone with the storm and the unreasoning terror. The radio beeped annoyingly again, but the warnings hadn't changed.

"I need something hot to drink," he said. "Can I get you anything?"

He would disappear again, and she decided she wasn't going to allow that for even as long as it took to make a pot of coffee. Sitting here waiting for her roof to cave in, ridiculous as it was to anticipate such a thing without a tornado, wasn't helping at all.

She pushed herself up and followed him to the kitchen. There she insisted on making the coffee herself, and he didn't protest, as if he understood her need to do something.

"I'm sorry I ran out like that," he said.

"I'm sorry I made you. I was poking my nose into things I know nothing about."

"No, actually, I think what got to me was that you might be right."

She turned to look at him. He pushed a chair out from the table. "Sit," he said. "Please. Let me get the hassock for you."

"I'm okay for a few minutes." But as the coffee began to heat behind her, she decided to sit anyway.

He spoke again. "You know, that barn of yours needs some work or it'll collapse in a few years."

She nodded, uncertain about where he wanted to take this but figuring it was well past time to keep her mouth shut.

"It's a good barn," he went on. "Useful. I'd hate to see you lose it."

"Someday," she said finally. "A lot of things are on a someday status right now. Like Linda Marie's nursery."

He nodded. "I was out there thinking. Watching the rain fall inside. It kills me to see something like that. I get all itchy to fix it."

At that she gave him a small smile. "It offends you?"

"I guess you could say that. But it helped me realize something and so you were right. I'm taking too much on my shoulders because I'm a control freak and I hate to feel helpless. Doesn't mean I won't keep on doing it, doesn't mean I won't keep blaming myself for Brandy, but there it is. Now you know my worst flaws. Well, I think they're the worst. Hell, I wasn't even happy as a contractor because I had to trust other people too much."

"So if you could do anything you wanted now, what would it be?"

"Cabinetry. Skilled, detailed, and very much under my control. Hell, I'd even get to draw up the plans instead of following someone else's."

"Then do it. At least you can." She sighed. "I'm in kind of a bovine state right now."

"Meaning?"

"Placid in a lot of ways, although maybe you haven't been able to tell. My doc says it's normal that I can't seem to look beyond the birth. I need to stay as calm as possible for the baby. She did warn me I'd probably go on a cleaning binge a few days or weeks before labor, but in the meantime I'm essentially a broody hen sitting on her egg. I should be making plans, figuring out what I'm going to do after Linda Marie arrives, thinking about jobs and all that stuff. But it doesn't keep my attention for long. It's as if there's this red-letter day coming and nothing else matters really."

She sneaked a look at him and found his expression warm. "Anyway, at least you're in a position to change your whole life and make decisions. I'm just waiting."

"You're waiting for something very important that's going to shake your whole life up. How can you make plans until you know everything's okay and what it's like to be a mom?"

"Good question."

The coffee finished but he insisted they drink it in the living room where she could put her feet up. Since the warnings on the radio hadn't changed except for more detailed information about the areas at risk for flash flooding, he turned it off, saying, "We can check again a little later."

She was glad to have the noise gone and in its absence to be able to tell the storm had weakened. She hoped it kept weakening.

He spoke into a silence that felt as if it were growing awkward. "We'll get your roof done in the morning if the weather holds."

And then he'd leave. He'd pick up his backpack and take off for California. She regarded the prospect with aching dismay, a dismay she wouldn't have believed herself capable of feeling when she had picked him up on the roadside. It was way too early to be feeling that his absence was going to leave a big hole in her life. She hadn't even felt that when Jeff died.

She closed her eyes and reminded herself she had been doing just fine until Ryder had arrived. If anything, she was better off now because she'd met some of her neighbors and they seemed to be caring people. It would be all right.

She only wished she believed that.

They dined on leftovers from lunch. This time Marti didn't argue about doing the dishes but let Ryder do it. What he'd said about being a control freak and feeling helpless with Brandy had struck home with her. If it made him feel better to do dishes, then there was no reason to argue.

After dinner, the storm picked up steam, rumbling loudly and dumping rivers of rain. They checked the radio again, but the warnings remained the same.

"From what I understand," Marti remarked, "this place isn't really built for floods. And with all the rain over the past few days, the ground must be saturated."

"Good for sheep grazing," Ryder remarked, reminding them of their conversation earlier with Ransom and his son.

"But maybe for nothing else."

He switched off the radio again and hesitated. She wondered what he was thinking, why he hesitated so visibly. Something that would make her uncomfortable?

Then he spoke. "You said something about the nursery being a 'someday' thing. What's it like?"

He'd definitely hit on one of her favorite preoccupations, even if she couldn't do much about it. "It's far from finished," she answered. "Do you want to see it?"

"I'd like to, actually."

"I'm warning you, you'll be distinctly unimpressed." But she led the way upstairs anyway, to the place in this house that truly held her biggest dream for the future. He followed, carrying both a flashlight and an oil lamp.

The room was in the middle of the upstairs hall, near the bathroom and over the living room. She threw the door open and let him lead the way in with the lights.

"See? Nowhere near done."

It almost embarrassed her to let someone else look at her meager preparations: the ad hoc changing table with a row of baby oil, baby powder and a box of disposable diapers. A tube of diaper rash ointment. A minuscule hair brush. The small travel bassinet opened on the floor, covered with tiny sheets. The open drawer in which she'd managed to stash a few bits of clothing. Walls that needed paint or paper.

It was definitely a minimum.

"It actually looks like a good start," he remarked. "What else do you envision in here?"

"Paint. Maybe wallpaper but that seems way more expensive. A crib. Some cheerful curtains."

"You're not asking for much."

"How much is for the baby and how much for me?"

At that he flashed a smile. "It's mostly for you," he agreed. "Nothing wrong with that. But it'll have an effect on Linda Marie, too. That's what you're thinking."

"Are you mind reading?"

"Maybe." He surprised her by putting the oil lamp down on the dresser alongside the flashlight. Then he came to stand behind her, as if trying to see it from her perspective.

She thought it was adequate but absolutely no more than that.

He slipped his arms around her, warming her instantly with his strength and body heat. "Long ago," he said, "when I still had a social life, women used to have baby showers. I was never invited to one, but I heard about them anyway, benighted male that I am."

She gave a little laugh. "Well, I don't know anyone here so I'm on my own with this."

He rubbed one of his hands over her belly, as if caressing the baby. "So can I be a sort of uncle and do a bit about it? I mean, I'm starting to take a very personal interest in Linda Marie. I think she likes me, too. She kicks me."

Another giggle escaped her, but then she turned within the circle of his arms to face him. "Ryder, you don't have to solve all my problems."

"I figured that out when I was in the barn. I couldn't anyway, being only one ordinary guy. But I can do a mean coat of cheerful paint in an afternoon, if you'll just choose a color. You shouldn't breathe the fumes anyway."

Feeling inexplicably shy, she drew away and went to the dresser. "This is my dream room," she murmured. "It's like my whole future revolves around this. So I spend a lot of time dreaming in here." She reached into the second drawer and pulled out paint chips and wallpaper samples. She offered them to him. "As you can see, I dream big when I let myself."

He took them and fanned his way through them using the whiter light of the flashlight. "This doesn't look terribly big to me. It's certainly a job you can't do yourself, but it's really not that big. How about putting wallpaper on either the upper or lower half—although the upper half would be more practical—and paint on the other half?"

"I've thought about it." She pulled together a paint sample and a wallpaper sample. "I liked this combination."

"That's a good one. I like the minty greens, and the little stuffed animals are cute."

She lifted them, admiring them together, then sighed and put them back in the drawer. "Someday," she said.

"Someday," he agreed as he gently patted her bulging tummy. "Only the best for Linda Marie."

She laughed at last, letting go of the wistfulness she always felt in here. "The sky's the limit," she agreed. Then she paused. "Why should you care about my baby?"

"I just do. I'm developing some affection for that baby bump. Maybe because it seems so special and I could never have one of my own."

She thought that over as the storm raged outside while it remained cozy inside. That was sad, she decided, but she could understand it when his wife had been so sick. Still, it had evidently pained him not to have a family.

Then she had a stray idea that disturbed her. She hoped he wasn't looking after her just because of the baby.

Because if he just wanted to play the role of a father for a few days, that might wound her more than his departure.

Chapter 7

Claiming to be trying to find his brother's wife had gotten Ben some very complete directions to the ranch owned by the Marti Chastain Ryder had mentioned.

God, who would want to live in this desolate place? After he left that podunk town that called itself a city, he rarely saw human habitation. Plenty of fences, yeah, some of them falling down, but not houses. Talk about the ends of the Earth!

He saw the tornado track, too, and was reluctantly impressed. They had their weather problems where he lived, too, but nothing like that sweeping path of destruction that looked like some giant vacuum had traveled for miles over the landscape.

The roads had been cleared of debris, but now it was simply stacked in drainage ditches by the road, ditches now full of water. Telephone and power poles were still bent and twisted here and there, and he passed some crews working on them.

What a mess.

But, he decided, with everyone preoccupied by the storm's aftermath, no one would be paying attention to one guy just driving through, even if he did have Nevada plates on his rental. And that cover story had been a stroke of genius. Nobody had questioned whether Marti Chastain's late husband had a brother.

Apparently they didn't know her very well. Another reason to cheer.

He began to realize he had a problem, though, when he drew near the woman's place and saw how little cover there was for him and the car. Hell. He needed to be able to figure out the setup before he acted, and it would be all to the better if he could get Ryder alone.

It wasn't going to be easy.

Not that he cared if he had to take out the woman, too. If she proved to be an obstacle, she'd be moved. Or dead. The important thing was to make Ryder pay for Brandy.

He reached the turn for the Chastain place and saw a house in the distance, almost concealed in a dip. And no place to hide a car.

Damn. He kept going another mile, and wonder of wonders he found a huge stand of trees, leafing out with spring leaves. He was able to jockey the car into a place where he couldn't be seen from the road.

Then he pulled out what he needed from the trunk—binoculars, that big old hunting knife he'd shoplifted so it couldn't be traced to him, some gloves and a jacket. A couple of water bottles, too, and he reminded himself to carry them out with him.

Leave no trace. He hadn't been in the military for

long before they'd tossed him, but he'd learned enough about surreptitious approaches and observation. Too bad they'd thought he'd enjoyed the prospect of being a sniper too much. He'd have thought they'd have welcomed that. Apparently not.

He still wasn't sure what exactly he'd done wrong, but he'd never forgotten the look on the face of the two officers who'd given him the word and had hustled him through medical discharge at light speed.

He shrugged mentally. It didn't matter anymore. What mattered was getting Ryder.

Certain he was equipped for a clean kill that would leave no trace, he started hiking back to the Chastain place.

And what he saw there through his binoculars only made him madder. Ryder was hugging that woman right on her front porch in plain sight.

Oh, yeah, he was going to enjoy ridding the world of that guy.

The roof had been finished two days ago, and Ryder was still hanging around. He was cutting up the felled trees into cord wood for her stove and stacking it neatly out back. He puttered with other things, too, and Marti began to think he was reluctant to resume his journey.

But now he was going to town to get some things he said he needed, and he didn't invite her along. At some deep level that bothered her, but then he hugged her and told her he wouldn't tarry. He also told her not to cook because he was going to bring home a meal.

He surprised her by hugging her before he left. For the past couple of days he had avoided touching her, and she suspected he was doing so because of the unmistakable sexual tension that kept growing between them.

Of course he didn't want to do something that might make him feel worse about Brandy in some way. In fact, were Marti to be honest, she had to admit she was beginning to resent Brandy. That woman had caused a nice man a whole lot of pain, the kind of pain that made him pull back from another woman.

It was as if Ryder had developed a phobia almost like the one she had over thunderstorms…except he had a lot more cause for it.

She watched him drive away, feeling almost abandoned, then stood looking out over the prairie to the blue-tinged mountains to the west. Nothing had changed, she argued to herself. Nothing at all. She'd been fine before Ryder, and she'd be fine after Ryder.

But she sure wished he'd get over his hangup before he left because she was growing increasingly hungry for his absent touches. Increasingly eager to learn the sexual lessons he might be able to teach her. He was steadily restoring a piece of her womanhood that Jeff had taken away, and she wanted it back. Even if it was just a one-night stand.

But she couldn't find the words to express it, and the last time she had tried, Ryder had said she had just handed him a grenade. That, she thought, had been the beginning of his withdrawal. That and when she'd caused him to storm out into the rain.

Sometimes a guy could be just too nice, she thought with something between despair and amazement.

A wind blew up, causing her to feel chilled. As she turned to go back inside, though, she felt something that unnerved her even more. The back of her neck prickled with the sense that someone was watching her.

Rubbing her arms to ward off the chill, she turned to look back out over the fields and couldn't see a soul.

Must be an animal, she decided, then went inside to keep herself busy until Ryder returned.

Ryder hadn't wanted to take Marti with him because he hadn't wanted to listen to a bunch of objections. He had plans, and he knew she'd be embarrassed, reluctant and stubborn. He was starting to get the measure of her.

Plus, he wanted her. He wanted her like mad, until it dominated nearly every waking thought he had. He was long past wondering if it was okay to want a pregnant woman and deep into wondering if he was still too messed up to even think of such a thing.

But he was thinking about it, and he desperately needed a couple of hours away to try to clear his head and find some sort of path through a confusion Marti was only increasing.

Not that she meant to. She kept trying to tell him he was a good guy who was blaming himself too much, and he was beginning to think she was right.

So why all the confusion? Misplaced loyalty to Brandy? A desire to punish himself? Fear of losing control again by caring too much?

He needed a shrink.

Instead he had only himself and a few hours to try to think through exactly what he really wanted and whether it would be good for Marti—or for him.

Such a question shouldn't seem so complicated.

He reached town and started shopping. He had tucked those two samples in his breast pocket and bought paint and wallpaper for the nursery, along with rollers, brushes and all the other things he'd need that he hadn't found around the place.

He thought about the aging linoleum that covered wood floors throughout the house. That always offended him, to cover good wood with that stuff, but he guessed there'd been a point where someone had thought it would be easier to care for. Or maybe they'd succumbed to a trend.

But he left that for another time. Right now he just wanted to brighten the place and give Marti a piece of her dream. Everyone deserved a dream. Like him and going back to cabinet making.

At Freitag's Mercantile, he found a narrow selection but enough for what he wanted. A wooden crib he could paint to match the room if she liked. Bedding that looked good with the paint and wallpaper samples.

He was a completely out of his depth but found a middle-aged clerk who helped him through rows of baby clothes and accessories. The woman assured him that with a baby you could never have too much. He wondered if that was true or just a sales gimmick but decided to rely on the woman's kind nature.

He added a stack of receiving blankets, a real changing table, some cute infant outfits, and then called a halt.

He had a feeling he was going to face some wrath over this, but in the end he trusted that Marti's eyes were going to sparkle with delight and her dream would grow.

He stopped by Maude's to pick up a couple of her steak sandwiches, then headed back realizing that he hadn't sorted his head out one bit.

All he knew was he wanted to see Marti's eyes sparkle. Maybe that was the only answer right there.

When he set out for Ben's, he just needed to know that he'd left things better in his wake. They wouldn't be perfect, much as he wished he could make it so, but at least they'd be better.

He'd feel less helpless, even if he couldn't be in control.

As long as Marti didn't make him bring everything back, anyway.

When Marti heard her truck coming up the rutted drive, she jumped up and went to the door. Where once she'd loved being alone when Jeff went out for a few hours, now she found she hated it. Because Ryder wasn't there.

No amount of argument from her brain could change that, either, because she'd spent the past few hours arguing with herself.

She was walking into deep waters and couldn't seem to turn back. Her heart ached with anticipatory loss even as it leaped at Ryder's return.

Linda Marie seemed to be just as glad because she kicked a few times, hard enough in sensitive enough places to make Marti wince briefly.

"Settle down, girl," she told both herself and the baby. Neither of them were listening.

She stood on the porch as Ryder climbed out of the truck cab with a large paper bag.

"Lunch," he said cheerfully.

As he drew closer, she saw a smile in his eyes and felt pleasure warm her. He smiled so rarely, and it was an expression that delighted her when it made a rare appearance. She smiled back and saw his face brighten even more.

She liked it even better when he gave her a quick hug with one arm after they went inside to eat.

The foam containers had kept the sandwiches warm, and although one of them was more than she could eat, she figured Ryder would consume her other half. He worked hard and had a very healthy appetite. A healthy enough appetite that he even managed to make her simplest dinner offerings seem like gourmet meals.

"How was your trip to town?" she asked.

"You been in the Mercantile much?"

"Rarely. Just a few times."

"Well, there's this one clerk. Sweet lady. She helped me a whole lot. That's rare these days."

"I guess it is to judge by what I experienced before I moved out here. I can remember hunting for help and then getting very little of it." She wondered why he'd even gone there and why he had needed help, but she swallowed the questions. Lately it had seemed to her she might be talking too much and asking too many question. She had to learn to let him volunteer what he wanted to share with her. Not that she was going to get much of a chance to practice.

"Exactly. The only place I didn't have a problem was at the lumberyard. Anyway, they're working on the telephone and electric poles on the way out here. Maybe you'll have power and phone back soon."

"Did you call Ben?"

"I already told him it was going to be a couple of weeks, that I wasn't going to leave you in a lurch. He doesn't need to hear it again. And I already know he blames me."

"That's not right!"

"Maybe not. But maybe having him dump his anger all over me will do some good."

"How could that possibly do any good?"

His smile was crooked. "Maybe I need to fight back with something other than my own head."

She pondered that as she chewed another bite of her sandwich. "That might work," she said finally. "Arguing with ourselves isn't the same as arguing with someone else. Things sound different then."

"Especially if you hear stupidity pouring out of your own mouth."

She laughed quietly. "Especially then. But sometimes you can also hear the sense you're making."

"Sound like you've had some experience."

She paused, then just decided to admit it. "I argued with myself an awful lot about divorcing Jeff. Then I'd remember those marriage vows and I couldn't bring myself to break them."

"Sometimes there's good reason."

"Obviously. I wouldn't judge anyone else's situation. I just know where I got hung up every time. I think you understand, Ryder, because you didn't leave Marti, and I'm sure nobody would have blamed you if you had."

The silence seemed to last forever before he answered. "That played into it. But it wasn't all of it. I still loved her. She never mistreated me. So I never lost hope. I get the feeling it was a whole lot different for you."

"Plenty of verbal abuse," she admitted. "Enough to kill my feelings for him finally."

"That's a huge point of difference," he said quietly. "Huge. Mistreatment isn't included in the vows."

That caught her up short. "No, I guess it isn't. But I kept on thinking of it as part of his illness."

"We all have our blind spots. I'm certainly beginning to see some of mine."

He wrapped up the remains of their sandwiches for later, then smiled. "Ready for your baby shower?"

Surprise made her heart slam. "My what?"

"Come out to the truck."

Filled with nervous excitement, she followed him, and when he started to pull the tarp off the truck bed, she burst into tears.

"Aw, heck," he said. "I didn't mean to make you cry."

"These are happy tears, Ryder. I mean...why? Why did you do all this? And it must have burned a hole in your bank account... Oh, you shouldn't have!" She hiccupped as more tears started to run down her cheeks.

He turned and wiped them gently away with his thumb. "I was afraid you'd get mad."

"How could I get mad at so much generosity? But the expense!"

"Trust me, expenses aren't high on my agenda. I just sold a profitable business."

She stared at the crib box, the paint, the packages, then turned toward him, throwing her arms around his neck. "Thank you. Oh, thank you."

"I hope you like it all," he said a bit gruffly as he hugged her back. "The nice lady at Freitag's said you could never have enough for a new baby, so I don't know if I did enough or went overboard. But if you don't like something, I can take it back."

"I'm sure I'll love it all," she answered somewhere between a sob and a laugh. "How could I not?"

He insisted she get comfortable in the living room until he had carried everything upstairs, then she could open packages.

Sitting in her chair she watched him walk by and wondered what she had ever done to deserve the arrival of an angel in her life. Because he was an angel, the kind who tried to make things better, the kind who did what he felt needed doing. How many people were so blessed?

Just for a little while, she reminded herself. Just for a short time. Soon he'd head out and she'd be alone again.

But damn it, she thought with a touch of bravado, that didn't mean she couldn't enjoy him while he was here. She had long since learned everything in life cost something, and when Ryder moved on the price was going to be high emotionally. But she'd lived through a lot, if there was one thing she knew for certain, she was a survivor. She would make it.

In the meantime, she wasn't going to look a gift horse in the mouth. That would be rude and ungracious.

"Ready?" he called as he passed through with a hefty bag. "This is it."

Five minutes later she was sitting on a chair in the nursery and crying and laughing all at once. A beautiful crib still in its box. A changing table to be assembled. The generosity of it took her breath away. But then she started pulling things out of bags and her breath caught with pleasure and excitement.

With eyes and hands she devoured the soft pretty things, the impossibly tiny things, the stack of cute receiving blankets. Things she had actually looked at a couple of times and then walked away from. It was almost as if he'd figured out her taste just from a paint chip and wallpaper sample.

"Oh, Ryder," she said, again and again. "Oh, Ryder, thank you."

He was leaning against the wall with his arms folded,

looking pretty pleased with himself, and she liked that. He should feel that way more often.

"I'm just...overwhelmed," she whispered finally. "How can I ever thank you?"

"By enjoying it. Because I'm going to enjoy knowing you're enjoying it."

She looked at him with misty eyes. "It's so much!"

"I'm almost positive that clerk thought it was nowhere near enough. You're not mad at me?"

"How could I be?" She rose, letting the receiving blankets tumble onto one of the bags, and hurried toward him. Her foot caught on something and she started to fall.

But powerful arms caught her and saved her, and then she was wrapped in strength.

"God, you're beautiful," he said.

Before she could say anything, their eyes locked. Then his head dipped toward hers.

And some happy voice deep inside her said *yes!*

The sun had sunk behind the mountains, and Ben gave up his surveillance. The late afternoon was growing chilly and darker, and he had a pretty good idea that he wasn't going to get Ryder alone tonight.

He might have to change his plans somewhat, and that left a bad taste in his mouth. The woman seemed to be with him most of the time, and she was a witness. He didn't particularly care about having to kill her to protect himself, but leaving two bodies behind would draw a hell of a lot more attention. He was going to have to give this more thought, and more thought meant more time.

Cussing and irritated, he headed back across fields to

make sure his car still hadn't been noticed. He avoided the road even though traffic was lighter than he could ever have imagined traffic to be.

He didn't believe a single one of Ryder's excuses because he remembered Brandy as she had been before her marriage. She'd had a few bouts of the blues, but nothing so serious that she hadn't bounced back in a few days or weeks. To him it seemed obvious that Brandy's deterioration, which had begun about a year after the marriage, had to be directly linked to something Ryder had been doing.

Ben, by nature, was a man who liked the taste of revenge. He always found a way to get even and prided himself that his responses were proportional.

A life for a life in this case.

Taking that woman's life also would be out of proportion, but it didn't trouble him too much. Sometimes circumstances dictated a bigger response, and this was beginning to look like one of those instances.

Well, he could wait a few days and watch some more. Maybe he'd find an answer in the patterns of the things they did. As soon as he found that pattern, he would make Ryder bleed out the way his sister had. No gunshot to end it quickly. No, he was going to bleed to death. It was just unfortunate that slashing Ryder's wrists wouldn't do the job. Too complicated and too difficult, so it would have to be something more certain.

Like cutting his throat.

Imagining it kept Ben going all the way back to his car. It made him calmer as he pulled out a sleeping bag and curled up in the passenger seat with the back dropped all the way.

It filled his dreams much later when he at last slept.

Ryder owed him a life, the life of the only person Ben had ever really cared about. And like a loan shark, Ben was going to collect.

Ryder couldn't sleep. That kiss in the nursery had gone from gentle to passionate in one second flat. He'd forced himself to end it there because he didn't want Marti out of some misplaced sense of gratitude. The disgust he would have felt for himself would have flogged him for a very long time.

But he'd heard her response in her quickened breathing, felt it in the way she had clung and opened her mouth to him. Seen it in the hazy look in her eyes.

Now he was lying in the dark, his loins heavy and aching in a way that was going to keep him up half the night.

For a long time now, he'd lost these feelings. He'd had to bury them because Brandy was never in the mood and he didn't want to make her feel any worse over anything.

He'd built a wall around her, he realized, protecting her from everything. He brought no problems home with him, he'd done all the cooking and cleaning and everything else, and he'd even taken responsibility for ensuring she took her meds.

Maybe he'd added to her depression by making her feel useless. He'd never know now, though, and he was getting tired of asking himself questions that had no answers.

The desire that had begun the very instant he set eyes on Marti wasn't helping clear his thoughts anyway.

That was a question with an answer.

All he had to do was walk down the hall and ask.

Or get in her truck and see if there were any easy

women in town. No, he realized instantly, that wouldn't make him feel any better. It never had.

What he wanted was Marti. Why the hell was he making it so complicated? She knew he was just passing through. If she welcomed him, it meant that she was prepared to accept that. Simple questions, simple answers.

Somehow it all seemed tangled up anyway.

Ah, hell. He gave up and wandered the roads of fantasy he'd been denying himself for so long. Marti would be beautiful naked, although he doubted she would believe it right now. He had no trouble imagining her lying on her bed, her pregnancy merely adding to a womanliness that he'd detected from holding her in his arms.

Full firm breasts, fuller because of her pregnancy, probably pale and blue-veined to judge by her light skin. A thick thatch of blond hair between her thighs beckoning him.

He imagined turning her around so that she lay on the edge of the bed so he could love her without hurting Linda Marie. He imagined her sighs, her moans, her pleasure, and with each imagined sound his passion mounted until he was so heavy with need he almost groaned.

Parting her petals, running his fingers over her most sensitive and private parts, learning her most intimate secrets. Bending over her to carefully suck at her nipples.

He touched himself, and felt his body leap. It had worked in the past when his needs had been unanswerable and too big to ignore.

But this time he stopped, realizing that another solitary orgasm wasn't going to ease his real need for a woman, a particular woman.

Somehow the need was making a joke out of all his reasoned reluctance. How much would he really hurt the lady with a single night of ecstasy? Good question.

Maybe he could just give them both a great memory to store up for the days and months ahead. He sure as hell knew the importance of memories like that, because they'd helped him through the worst of times with Brandy.

Memories of good things. They added up to the reason people kept on living. If all you had were memories of bad things, what would be the point?

He'd seen how Marti had responded. Maybe she wanted it as much as he did. Maybe she even needed it to realize that she was definitely an attractive, sexy woman.

Maybe he was doing them both a disservice by fighting something that was almost tangible between them. By the way she had kissed him back earlier, he was sure his feelings were reciprocated.

So why be a damn fool and deny them both what they wanted?

The next thing he knew, he was standing outside Marti's bedroom door, wearing nothing but his shorts.

He was going to explode if he didn't love that woman. It was as simple as that.

Chapter 8

Marti heard Ryder stir. At first she thought he was going to the bathroom, but his steps came down the creaky hall floor and stopped by her bedroom.

Oh, please come in, she thought as her body gave in to all the cravings he had awakened in her. All the things she'd tried not to think about even as her body had been sending loud and furious signals almost from the outset.

Fantasies she hadn't allowed herself to have suddenly burst into her mind full-blown, as if they'd been rehearsed at some subconscious level. Ryder's hands and mouth on her, learning every single inch of her, possessing her at last.

Oh, how she wanted his possession. Every cell inside her seemed ready for it. Between her legs, a deep aching throb resumed, a throbbing that had never been far away since he had arrived.

He'd been so careful of her, so cautious, and too damn gentle. She was sure she wouldn't break, and she so desperately needed to feel wanted, if only for a single night.

It had been so long since she'd been really wanted or made to feel truly sexy. An eternity had passed since her body had awakened the way this man awakened it with a few kisses and touches.

Sometimes she felt he was the key to her lock.

Ridiculous, she tried to tell herself as she listened to the silence. She bit her lip and stirred restlessly as deepening desire took command.

She threw back the blankets as her own internal heat took over the job. Lying there in a simple nightshirt, surely the least sexy thing ever devised, she wished she had some beautiful peignoir, some lacy piece of something to enhance her appeal.

She wished she could find voice to call out to him. But hanging on the thread of taut anticipation, she awaited his decision. Because she really didn't believe in her own appeal, rejection would be the worst thing of all.

The night, though chilly, seemed to have grown sultry. She began to breathe harder as if all the air were being sucked from the room.

She didn't know if she could stand the anxious expectancy.

Then the door opened with a creak, and she heard Ryder say quietly, "Marti?"

All she could manage was, "Hmm?"

"Are you awake?"

Never more awake in her life. "Yes." A bare whisper.

He entered the room but left the door open behind him as if he didn't plan to stay. Her hopeful heart began to sink, but the rest of her remained wired on the most basic of needs.

He approached on surprisingly light feet. There wasn't enough star shine coming through the window to make him any more than a dark shadow. All of a sudden she wished for light so she could see him.

She felt him perch on the bed beside her, heard the springs creak beneath his weight. "If I stay," he said quietly, "I'm going to make love to you. I don't want to do that if it will hurt you. So tell me, do I stay or go?"

She wondered almost crazily if he meant he'd leave permanently. But what did it matter? She had only one answer anyway. "Stay."

Thank goodness he didn't ask if she was sure. She wanted no more pointless questions to interrupt the magic building inside of her and flowing between them. It did indeed feel like magic, as if a spell of desire had wrapped around her, had wrapped them in a private cocoon.

He didn't hesitate any longer. He stretched out beside her and slipped an arm beneath her shoulders, drawing closer.

She almost gasped with delight as she realized he wore next to nothing. At that instant, nothing could have stopped her from running her hands over his warm, smooth skin. Her palms were eager for the feel of him, wanting to learn his every inch.

Smooth muscles responded to her touches as she traced his chest and then finally managed to get on her side so she could run her hand over his back. More muscles, and they leaped at her touch in the most pleasing way.

He seemed to welcome her eagerness and reciprocated. Even as his mouth settled over hers for a deep, possessive kiss, he began to claim the rest of her with his hands. She wasn't aware that her nightshirt had bunched up around her shoulders until she felt his warm hands begin to caress her bare breasts.

Impossibly, excitement leaped even higher in her very depths. Each brush of his palms and fingers set a new fire burning. Her nipples grew huge and more sensitive than she had ever guessed they could. Even the lightest of his touches seemed to leap to her very center until she felt as if a welder's arc ran from them to her core. And with each touch, she throbbed more strongly.

His tongue tangled with hers, a knowing tongue that timed itself perfectly with the way her hips seemed to tighten. She lifted a hand, trying to draw his head closer but instead felt him pull away. Too fast, too soon.

But then his mouth found her breast, at first just licking her, driving her crazy with a need for stronger touches, deeper touches. But not until her hips lifted a little did he answer her silent plea, drawing her nipple deeply into his mouth, flicking it with his tongue even as he sucked on it.

A low, helpless moan escaped her. Nothing in her life had ever prepared her for feelings this intense or a pinnacle so high. She felt dizzy with it, as if she were already teetering on the pinnacle and ready to tip over.

So hot, so quick, so strong. Never had she ignited this way before. The thrill carried her to a newly discovered landscape of hunger.

She hated that she couldn't move freely, that even twisting onto her side was difficult now that he was there. She tried to find purchase to roll over even more so she could meet him directly, but he stilled her quickly with his hand.

"Don't struggle," he murmured, finding her mouth with his again. "I'll help."

Regretting the loss of his hot wet mouth on her breast, she forced herself to still and cried out ecstatically when he began again to suck on her breast.

Then he caught her hand and drew it downward, wrapping it around his swollen staff.

The silky satin of his skin there unleashed another wave of longing. He felt so big, so hard, and it was all for her.

She murmured her delight incoherently and tried to stroke him. Then his fingers settled between her legs, parting her, opening her, caressing her lips lightly. He might as well have struck a match.

Her hand tightened around him. "Ryder..." The moan escaped her and he seemed to understand the words she couldn't voice.

"Easy," he whispered.

She almost cried out in protest when he drew back from her, but before she could find breath to protest, she realized he had risen from the bed. He was leaving.

Before her heart could plummet into the depths of disappointment and despair, however, she felt him lift her and turn her so her bottom rested on the edge of the bed with her legs dangling to the floor.

"We have someone else to care for," he murmured, his voice a little thick.

The thoughtfulness touched her heart but then he parted her legs, opening her widely to him. Shyness almost overwhelmed her and she was suddenly glad there was no light. She felt so exposed, and although it was a good feeling, it was a little scary, too.

But then he took that fear and turned it right back into passion. His fingers stroked her, circling in on that knot of nerves that had become almost painful with passion.

The lightest of touches on that nub, and she bucked almost violently. She never wanted it to stop, this pleasure-pain he was inducing.

It didn't stop. He continued until waves of hunger overwhelmed her like a tsunami.

Then, something else she had never experienced before. She almost froze as she realized what he was doing. His mouth was on her down there now, his tongue following the earlier path of his fingers. Hot, wet, silky.

Nature and need took over, causing her hips to rise and fall with each touch until she begged, "Ryder... Ryder..."

At last he straightened and slipped into her heated depths, slowly, so very slowly, as if he wanted them both to feel every inch of his penetration.

When he moved, it was with a gentleness that was at once maddening and arousing. Gently, gently, his thrusts continued, each one lifting her even higher.

Dimly she was aware of his heavy breathing. Her own panting sounded loud in the room. The panting became helpless moans.

Please, please, please...

The orgasm rolled through her like an endless rumble of thunder, shaking her entire body, endlessly intense. She almost felt as if she exploded, as if the entire night turned blindingly brilliant. She felt him jerk, heard him groan and stiffen.

She tipped over the edge into an abyss of release and pleasure she had never before known.

And when it was done, he leaned over her on his elbows and let his head fall gently on her breasts.

It may have been a few minutes later, or it might have been an hour. She had lost all sense of time. Ryder turned her and covered her, then padded quickly from the room. She heard water in the bathroom, then the floor creaked at his return.

He surprised her. Saying nothing, he pulled back the covers and began to run a warm washcloth over her from her breasts down to the still tender and achy place between her legs.

It was such a caring gesture, she felt her eyes prickle but refused to give in to silly tears. He might misunderstand.

Before she could chill, the blankets had been drawn over her again, but this time he was under them with her. He helped her turn onto her side, then spooned himself against her back.

"Thank you," he said softly in her ear.

A long sigh of release and happiness escaped her. "Thank you."

His chuckle was quiet. "We could argue about that I suppose." His hand gently caressed the mound of her belly. "Passenger okay?"

"She's very okay."

"Good." He continued his gentle, soothing massage of her tummy, then allowed his hand to venture up to her breasts. Amazingly, she felt the heat of response again. So quickly.

"I protected you," he added. "I thought you should know that."

"What? Oh." She had trouble focusing. "Obviously I can't get pregnant."

"I don't have any disease," he explained, "but I didn't want to leave you wondering."

At those words the entire night seemed to darken more. He didn't want to leave her wondering. Referring to his departure, of course. She caught herself just before she could tumble into despair. Enjoy the minute she was in, she reminded herself. Don't ruin this by worrying about tomorrow or next week. Treasure it.

She sighed and stretched a little and felt his arms curl around her. Those arms seemed to cherish her and protect her, though she needed no protection at the moment. That didn't prevent her from liking it.

Her toes curled with contentment, then their feet tangled together.

"Lady," he said, "you are one spectacular lay."

The unexpected and unusual compliment completely banished the presentiment of anticipated sorrow. She giggled. "I've never been called a 'lay' before."

"Your education is sorely lacking," he replied, then emitted a quiet chuckle. "All right, you're a spectacular lover. Sexy as hell. I've been going out of my mind wanting you."

She liked the sound of that. "I didn't do all that much."

"All you have to do is breathe. Or smile. And say yes."

Another giggle slipped out. "I'll keep that in mind."

He passed his hands over her, his touch now as possessive and familiar as it was gentle. "I hate to ruin the moment, but I'm starving. Want me to bring a small picnic up here?"

"Sure. That sounds like fun. And some light. I'd actually like to see you."

"Ah, lady, the games have only begun. But I need to get my strength up. Besides, I'm almost positive that a growling stomach wouldn't enhance the mood."

She was still smiling almost giddily when he slipped out of bed and pulled his shorts on. And oddly, she felt younger than she had in a great many years.

She managed to pull some pillows around and push herself in a semi-sitting position while she waited. When Jeff had used to slip out of this bed, she hadn't missed him at all and had often hoped he wouldn't hurry back. Ryder's absence made the bed feel way too big and empty.

Later, she told herself. She'd deal with that later, but not before she absolutely had to.

She glanced toward the window and thought she saw a light out in the fields. As soon as she blinked it was gone.

The wind must have moved a remaining piece of debris, she decided. But then she remembered how earlier she had felt watched. For some reason, she thought of the shotgun in her closet. It had been Jeff's father's, and they'd taken it out for target shooting a few times. As soon as it crossed her mind, she pushed the memory away.

Why in the world would anyone be watching this house? Hormones, she told herself. Her hormones were just acting up, creating strange notions. She'd been living here alone for months now, and the only thing she had ever feared was taking a fall and being unable to get to the phone.

No reason to worry about anything else. This damn county was so safe as to be boring. However, she decided she wanted those curtains closed, even if there was nothing beyond that window except miles of empty land.

Sighing at her own silliness, she rose and pulled the curtains closed, then climbed back under the covers and against the pillows.

Only a few minutes later, Ryder returned with a large tray and an oil lamp. The flashlight beside her bed would have worked, but she'd used it so often since the power went out, she wasn't sure it would last long, and who wanted to be hunting for batteries in the dark?

He set the lamp down on her dresser, left the flame adjusted low to a dim, warm glow, then joined her on the bed with the plate of cheese and crackers. From the tray he passed her a tall glass of milk.

And since he lay atop the blanket, she got an eyeful. A very sexy eyeful. He had the kind of muscles a man got from hard physical labor, and he had a lot of them everywhere. Not bulging or eye-catching but clearly defined powerful muscles.

"My God," she said, "you have a six pack. How in the world did you manage that?"

He shrugged. "Genetics, I guess. As long as I work, it's there."

She couldn't resist. She put her milk aside and reached out to run her hand over his abdomen. "Some men would kill for this."

"I know. I've listened to enough of them moan. It's just the way I'm built."

She smiled and withdrew her hand. "Not vain, huh?"

"What's to be vain about? Like I said, it's genetics, and all I have to do is work. No gym necessary. Now if I'd spent thousands of hours and dollars somewhere trying to achieve that, I'd have something to be vain about."

An unusual way of looking at it, she thought. Her gaze trailed down his legs—gorgeous legs—and she was quite sure she'd never seen a finer figure of a man.

"You're eye candy," she announced.

That cracked him up and he almost choked. He grabbed a napkin to cover his mouth until it settled down, then he balled the napkin up and grinned at her. "You're the eye candy," he assured her.

She shook her head.

"Aww, don't give me that. You have very nice breasts."

"They're larger because of the pregnancy."

"What makes you think I'd like them any less if they were smaller?" He put the plate aside and brushed each nipple once with his thumb. "Saucy, too. Legs that go on for miles. Very nice legs. But mostly I like your smile. You have a smile that lights the place up."

The last compliment meant the most. "I like your smile, too," she agreed. "And I love your laugh. You don't laugh enough."

His smile faded a bit and she wanted to kick herself. "You're right," he admitted. "It's something I need to learn to do again. Soon."

"I'm sorry." She wished she would stop blurting out every thought that popped into her head. For years with Jeff she'd been able to swallow plenty of words, but with Ryder they just came out.

"No need," he assured her. "I stopped laughing quite a while ago. Nothing very much seemed funny. However—" he paused to pass her the plate so she could take another piece of cheese and a cracker "—I seem to be finding it a bit easier lately."

"Good." Then she bit the cracker and cheese to shut herself up. A shower of crumbs tumbled down onto her bare breasts. "Darn," she said through a full mouth.

"Sheets wash," he reminded her. "Well, they will once the power comes on again. But there are other methods of cleanup."

Before she could guess what he was about, he leaned over her and begin to lick the crumbs away. One of her hands still held the cracker, but the other was free to stroke his soft hair.

"Hmm," she said, "this could turn into an X-rated movie."

"Would that be so bad?" he asked as he licked another crumb away. "Don't wiggle, I'll lose some of them."

Her laugh gave way to a sigh. She watched as he lifted his head from time to time to seek another crumb, then licked her skin as if she were a cat.

"Definitely X-rated," she mumbled. Only a short time ago that same tongue had been doing some pretty wicked things to her, especially between her legs where not even Jeff had expressed any interest in kissing her. It wasn't that she didn't know people did that, it had just never happened to her.

She definitely wanted to try it again, but she didn't want to do a thing that would stop the glow that he was building at that moment.

Then he sat back and winked at her. "Eat another cracker so I can get back to work."

"You work too much."

"Ah, but we both enjoy some of it."

She laughed again and realized she was almost giddy

with satisfaction, pleasure and feeling cherished. Almost dizzy with delight. Places long kept locked away were awakening to the possibility of living again, and now she had a metric for knowing what she wanted in a man.

Ryder.

Oh, hell. Another thing she couldn't afford to think about. Some nasty little voice in her head reminded her there would be hell to pay emotionally when he left, but she decided it would be worth the price. This one night alone was worth every bit she would pay for it.

Well, she had a lot of practice with not thinking about tomorrow. Living in the moment. There had been no other way to deal with Jeff most of the time.

"Cracker, my lady? Or a tidbit of cheese?"

She almost skipped the cracker, then remembered the delight caused by the crumbs of the last. She didn't want to miss that.

He watched expectantly, then grinned as a couple of crumbs took a tumble. "I think I'm beginning to love crackers," he remarked. "They might become one of my favorite things to eat in bed."

"Until you try to sleep and roll over on them," she said, pretending to be serious. But seriousness didn't survive long past the first soft lick of his tongue.

"Ryder," she finally moaned.

"I know, I know," he said huskily. "Believe me, I know. But I refuse to rush."

"You can be so difficult!"

"I'm working on it," he agreed.

Then, slowly, once the last of the crumbs were gone, he took her to the stars again.

But this time he encouraged her to lead. To touch him however she wanted, let her see the power she had over him with the least caress. She got to see him writhe the way she had writhed, and between the freedom to touch him in any way that occurred to her and his responses, she surfed the cresting wave right alongside him.

She discovered that a man's nipples could be almost as sensitive as her own. So she sucked him the way he had sucked her, and heard his moans with satisfaction and deep pleasure.

Then, wanting to give him what he had given her, she clasped his erection and took him into her mouth. Jeff had liked that, too, but never before had she enjoyed doing it. Ryder's response to the intimacy, the way he bucked and groaned, was all it took to change her attitude.

His hand gripped her head, guiding her gently, teaching her the touches he liked best. She'd have been glad to continue forever, but Linda Marie chose that moment to kick a tender place inside her and she gasped.

At once Ryder stopped her and turned her back onto her side. "What?" he demanded. "Are you okay?"

"The baby. She just joined the romp."

A slow smile spread across his face. "I thought you said it doesn't hurt."

"Usually. Every so often she seems to find a nerve."

"Tsk," he said jokingly, and reached down to pat her belly. "Settle down, girl. You'll get your turn to be center stage in a few months."

Another laugh escaped Marti, but it concealed disappointment. She hadn't wanted to stop. She had wanted to know exactly what it was like to bring Ryder to orgasm by herself.

But apparently she hadn't stopped anything. He rolled

her onto her side so they were spooned together, and she felt his stiffened staff slip between her legs.

"There are other ways," he said and slipped his hand down to stroke her sensitive bundle of nerves that was already swelling with hunger.

"Plenty of other ways," he murmured again as he began to rock himself against her in time with his stroking fingers.

Yes, indeed, she thought as she lay exhausted a short time later. There were plenty of other ways.

Chapter 9

The morning brought an early summer glory that seemed appropriate after the night just passed. The sky glowed its most brilliant blue, and puffy white cumulus clouds dotted it. Unfortunately, they probably promised a storm later in the day, but Marti didn't care. She didn't care much except that the beauty of the day fit her mood.

She and Ryder worked together making a breakfast that would suit them both. Toast for her, because her stomach insisted that the morning sickness must continue, and eggs and some ham for him.

While they were cooking, the power turned on again, signaled by lights going on. They flickered a few times, then stabilized. "Hallelujah," Marti remarked.

"Darn, now I'm going to have to get used to doing things the easy way again."

She laughed. This morning she very much wanted to laugh about everything.

"I'll go make sure the generator has turned off. After breakfast. Why don't we take this outside since it's so beautiful?"

She liked that idea but didn't expect him to move chairs and a card table out onto the porch. Expected or not, that's exactly what he did. Soon they were seated side by side looking out over a world that, for the first time since the tornado, actually seemed to be full of promise.

"You need some rocking chairs out here," he remarked. "And don't tell me because I know. That's on the Someday List."

"That's right."

"However, for some things someday is today."

"Meaning?"

"I'm going to paint and paper the nursery. It's a good day for open windows so you won't breathe anything you shouldn't, and if the day stays dry I could be done by dinner tonight."

"So fast?"

"It doesn't take long. I've done a lot of it. Maybe tomorrow I can assemble the crib and the changing table. Or I can finish cutting up those trees, but right now I don't want to pass up a good chance to paint and paper."

She felt again that flicker of guilt that he was doing so much for her, but she really couldn't argue. She knew she couldn't do any of it herself, not even the painting, until after the baby was born. Not until she managed to find a job of some sort.

Or maybe part of what was bothering her was that

with each task he completed, she felt his departure loom closer.

She stole a glance his way and found him looking happier than she'd ever seen him. So maybe she was giving him something, too. A little peace. Certainly some great sex, although she didn't think that was quid pro quo with him. He certainly hadn't made her feel as if it was.

So maybe fixing things was good for him psychologically. She could get that because feeling helpless about so many things had been making her miserable.

"I can hardly wait to be useful again," she remarked. "Like painting. I can paint. I ought to be able to help you."

"I'm sure you can, but I don't know about the fumes. It's latex paint, reasonably benign, but I don't want to take a chance."

"I know." She sighed. "Maybe with the windows open?"

He thought for a moment. "You got a fan? Maybe if we can keep the air moving enough you can help. And then later I could enjoy washing the paint off you. With hot water even."

Her cheeks flamed like the sun, hot and obvious. He laughed and leaned back in his chair. "Yeah, that would be the best part," he agreed. "Assuming you don't object."

"Why in the world would I object?"

"Because a lady is always allowed to change her mind."

Amazingly, her cheeks grew even hotter.

But he switched subjects then, as if he didn't want to bring things to a head too soon.

"I bought some chair railing," he said.

"What's that?"

"You've seen it, I'm sure. It runs about chair height along a wall so you can't damage the wall."

"Oh, right."

"In this case, I figure it's the perfect thing to put along the line between wallpaper and paint. It'll cover the seam. Sound good to you?"

"Sounds perfect." The man thought of everything.

Then that odd sensation returned, the feeling of being watched. She looked out over the fields again, squinting, trying to see.

"What's wrong?"

"Probably hormones or something. Yesterday I felt like someone was watching and now I'm feeling it again. Crazy. There's no one out there."

But he didn't treat it as if she were crazy. He stood and started scanning the hay fields.

"Ryder, it's just a feeling."

"Also one of the most reliable weird feelings humans get."

"But there's no reason for anyone to be out there. Maybe it's just some animal. A cow."

"I'd see a cow out there," he remarked. "Must be something smaller."

"Well, let's not worry about it. Obviously it's an animal."

After a few moments, he settled back down to eat his breakfast, although she sensed there was a new tension in him.

But it was nothing to worry about, not with Ryder here. If some freak wanted to watch her from a distance, he wasn't going to do anything while Ryder was around.

She didn't want to think about what might happen after Ryder left. And she didn't want to admit that those fields were starting to look a whole lot less friendly.

Ben lay down in the tall grass or whatever it was, flattening himself. What the hell was going on? Why had Ryder looked out here like he sensed something?

But he couldn't possibly know Ben was here. And no one else was around anywhere.

So maybe he'd been surveying whatever this crop was. Ben didn't think it was ordinary grass. It looked too cultivated and too uniform. So yeah, that must be what Ryder was doing.

Just to be safe, though, as soon as the two of them went back indoors, he crawled away and started back to his car. Might be a good day to be away from here. Or to change his vantage point. Come to think of it, he'd beaten a clear trail in that grass. If someone came looking, it would be obvious something had been crawling that way from the road.

So he changed tacks, choosing a different observation point from which he could watch the house and see if Ryder came out and found the crushed grass.

The sun rose, the day lengthened and absolutely nothing happened. So Ryder wasn't suspicious of anything.

Hell, there was no reason on earth he should be. He'd never expect Ben out here. Even so, he had no reason to be suspicious of Ben. Everything was set for them to meet in Fresno, and he was certain that he'd given Ryder no indication of how much he wanted his vengeance.

He thought of going to town to get a decent meal, then reminded himself he didn't want to be seen there again. Getting directions had been one thing, and as long as he never showed up again, the guy he'd talked to probably wouldn't even remember him.

Unless he killed that Chastain woman. Hell. He pounded his fist on the ground. He had to make sure to deal with this in a way that no one would remember some stranger had come by asking about Marti Chastain. Of course, if that guy remembered anything about him at all, it was going to be an average-looking guy who hadn't given his name and had been driving a car with Nevada plates.

He blew a deep breath and reminded himself there would be absolutely no reason for him to be directly linked to this place. No one knew Ben was here. No one.

He rolled over onto his back, looking up into the endless blue sky with its growing accretion of cottony puffs of cloud and decided he had to make up his mind about some things.

He might not care about killing that woman to get to Ryder, but the murder of a guy who was a stranger around here would lead the investigation in all sorts of paths that would benefit Ben. Killing the woman, not so much. But how much had Ryder told her about him?

Probably not a lot, he thought. He hadn't talked about his feelings or suspicions about Ryder to anyone, and Ryder had a whole lot more to hide. So if Ryder had mentioned him at all, it was probably in vague terms. Even so, if Ben changed his appearance a bit, she'd give a description that wouldn't fit him, and they'd be looking at Ryder's life back east for a killer.

Which was exactly what he wanted. Okay, so the woman was off the table unless he could find no other way. But there would be other ways. Ryder often went out to the barn. Catching him out there would be just the ticket.

And honestly, he thought virtuously, he really didn't want to kill the Chastain woman. A life for a life was one thing. Going overboard would be bad karma. Nor did he want to make another woman one of Ryder's victims. Best to avoid it entirely if he could. So as long as she had no idea who he was, he'd leave her be.

Deciding that was the best way to go, he made up his mind to get into that barn late tonight or tomorrow night. Catching Ryder alone out there day or night would solve all his problems.

Tomorrow night, he decided. Miserable as he was crawling around in all this grass, he was enjoying a certain sense of power over Ryder's life, enjoying the anticipation of his revenge at least as much as he would have anticipated the pleasure of a gourmet meal. Maybe more.

He couldn't be sure because he hadn't killed before. There'd been times he wanted to, but never before had he been goaded the way he had by Brandy's death.

It was as if her suicide were her last message, telling him that Ryder had failed her. She wouldn't have killed herself otherwise, of that he was sure. Ryder must have made her life intolerable and had most likely been responsible for Brandy's depression.

In fact, it had gotten so bad that he hadn't even been able to talk to her on the phone. Ryder had been the one who called him and told him what was going on. Ryder had always been the one to take his calls.

The more he had thought about it, the more he had begun to believe that Ryder had made his sister a virtual prisoner, cutting off all her contact with the outside world. He wasn't even sure he believed all Ryder's claims over the past couple of years that Brandy was getting proper treatment.

He could have just made that up. It still galled Ben that Ryder had so often said, "She doesn't want to talk on the phone." Why would Brandy not want to talk to her own brother?

That had given birth to his suspicions, and he sometimes got angry with himself for not having investigated. He felt stupid for believing that Brandy was just sick and Ryder was taking care of her.

But if he'd been caring for her, Brandy would still be alive. Her death had been her last cry for help, and he knew it was directed at him.

She might as well have pointed the finger at Ryder and said, "He's the one who turned my life into hell."

He just wished he could find a way to make Ryder bleed out as slowly as Brandy had.

With all the upstairs windows and doors open, Marti and Ryder judged the air circulation to be good enough that she wouldn't breathe too many fumes. He planted a floor fan in the doorway of the nursery, making sure the air flowed out the open windows.

Marti pulled on her oldest sweatshirt, but because she didn't want to ruin one of her only two pairs of pregnancy jeans, she left her legs bare. The sweatshirt came down far enough to be as modest as a bathing suit, and Ryder thought it was cute.

In fact, he stole a few minutes to hug and kiss her, running his hands over her bare legs and making outrageous promises about what he was going to do to those legs later when he washed them. He left her almost giddy with laughter and excitement.

She learned a lot as she helped him with a level and a plumb line. He seemed appreciative of how well the house was built. "After all these years, you'd expect the floors and the ceiling to be off-square, but they're not by much. That makes life easy."

"Why?"

"Because it would drive you seriously nuts to walk into a room where the chair rail looked as if it was at an angle to the ceiling or floor."

"I hadn't even thought of that!"

"Well, now you don't have to. The place isn't exactly level, but it's so close it won't bug you."

That seemed to please him greatly, and she supposed it would because he was a builder.

She held the plumb line while he leveled it, and then he let her snap it. She grinned when she saw the line of blue dust marking the wall. "That's a brilliant invention."

"It's a godsend."

He set her up on an old chair with a roller and a paint pan. "Don't worry about crossing the line here and there. If it happens to vanish, I'll just put another one up so I can line up the wallpaper. Have fun."

She did. She could see fine paint splatters of mint green paint begin to decorate her legs as she ran the roller on the wall, but she didn't care. After all, she had promises for what Ryder was going to do about that, and she didn't want to miss them.

"Ryder?" she asked as the pleasant rhythm of work began to made her feel relaxed and easy.

"Yeah?"

"How do you go into the cabinetry business? Does someone hire you?"

"I open my own shop. With any luck I'll find some

place to put a few things on consignment that'll draw other people to my door."

"Can people still afford stuff like that?"

"Depends on how wealthy I want to be."

"Meaning?"

"If I don't put a ridiculously high price on my labor, most things would be affordable. More expensive than that stuff you buy from factories and put together yourself, but the quality would make up for it. The wood isn't so far out of sight that I couldn't be reasonable. Why?"

"I was just wondering. I know I'd never be able to afford anything that's handmade, but I guess other people are better off. But would that mean you have to live in a city?" She asked the question dreading the answer. Damn, she knew he was leaving, so what did it matter where he went? Obviously he couldn't stay around here. There weren't enough wealthy people to need two hands to count them.

"I can live anywhere I want," he said after a moment. "As long as I can cart pieces around in a truck and find a place in reasonable distance to show off my stuff."

"That would be nice."

"I want to have my cake and eat it, too," he said lightly. Then, "Marti? What have you been thinking about doing after the baby comes?"

"Like I said, I can't seem to focus on it. I know I can keep on leasing the land every year, so it's not like I need to make a bundle." Although she was still worrying about whether the leases would pay out in the fall after the crop damage from the tornado. Nor would she blame a guy if he said his crop was ruined and he just couldn't afford to pay up.

"What did you use to do?"

"Jeff didn't want me to work."

"Ah. Before that?"

"I was going to junior college. I still hadn't figured out exactly what I wanted to do, but I was leaning toward some kind of medical technician. Medicine always fascinated me. I was thinking I could get a job as a technician, then maybe go for a nursing degree."

"But you never got that far."

"Obviously not." She sighed and put the roller in the pan, reaching back to rub her lower back.

Almost instantly, Ryder took over the task. "You need to lie down?"

"No, it's okay." As his thumbs found a particularly tense spot, she gave a little groan. "Right there. That's it."

"I could give you a head-to-foot back massage later."

All at once the piercing longing for him returned and she wished she wasn't covered in paint, that she could just seize his hand and drag him toward her bed.

Not right then but definitely later, she promised herself. She was going to get that massage and a whole lot more.

She was still smiling when they finished the painting.

By the time they started to lose the outside light, Ryder had put up the last of the wallpaper. She stood in the middle of the room, turning around and admiring it.

"It's perfect! Oh, Ryder, I love it."

"I'm glad," he answered simply as he watched her smile and clasp her hands together with pleasure. It had been years since he'd brought a look of that much happiness to Brandy's face.

But pleasing Brandy had never been simple. Marti,

however, was terribly easy to delight. He felt a tightness in his chest as he considered all the little things she had done without during her time with Jeff and since his death. The kinds of things most people enjoyed, from painting a room to fixing a meal together.

Of course, it was not as if he and Brandy had done such things together, at least not since their first apartment and the early days of their marriage. Then the depression had moved in with them, a third party in the midst of what should have been a private duet.

That depression had been like a living monster, never far away, always ready to attack. A diamond necklace wouldn't have given Brandy the joy that a simple paint and paper job had given Marti. Not that it was Brandy's fault. Hell, no. If he'd ever blamed Brandy for her illness, he'd have left.

But he couldn't deny how good it made him feel to have made Marti so happy with so little.

He kept his promise about washing the paint off her. After days of icy showers, the hot water felt good, almost as good as her satiny, soapy skin as he washed her. It would have been easy to give in to the passion she stoked in him, passion hotter than a coal fire, but even as she began to make little sounds that told him she was feeling the same, he kept his common sense.

"You're pregnant." He chuckled, a statement of the very obvious. "No fooling around in the shower. Too dangerous."

She pouted, but only for an instant. Only when he had her standing on the bath mat and had dried her off—taking his good sweet time about it as he retraced the hills and hollows that so appealed to him—did he climb back in and wash himself down.

Damn, the ache between his legs was heavy and sweet. He could hardly wait for later.

While she made dinner, he closed up the windows then started some desperately needed laundry for both of them. When he joined her in the kitchen, the night sky beyond the window had grown almost black, with a beautiful purple edging around the mountains. The clouds had not yet fulfilled their promise of rain, but they did a little while later, unloading a torrent. At least there was no thunder and lightning to torment Marti.

"I'll get to the chair rails tomorrow," he said while they ate. "Then we should be able to put together the furniture."

She was sitting there nibbling at fish and mixed vegetables with an almost dreamy smile on her face.

"Marti? What are you thinking?"

"How much picking up a stranger in a storm has changed my life."

"Oh." He looked quickly down, unsure if that was good or bad. He still had to get to Fresno, he still had to put pieces of himself back together. He hoped he wasn't going to be leaving pain in his wake. But maybe after Fresno…

He caught himself, stifling the thought. He'd found a lonely widow and he'd done a few things for her, things that made him feel better about himself. He couldn't think of it as anything more. Not yet. Maybe never. Caring about someone, as he'd learned the hard way, could carry the harshest of prices.

When he looked up again, he found Marti's expression had become an odd mixture he couldn't quite read. Sorrow? Happiness? What?

"I'm glad I ran across you," she said. "You might

as well know it. It's only been a short time and I know you'll be leaving soon, but you probably have no idea how much you've changed me."

"How?"

She shrugged and hesitated. "It's hard to explain. Before you came I was living in my little isolated outpost. I didn't want friends, I didn't want anything except Linda Marie. I'd pulled into a shell because of Jeff. I just hadn't realized how far I'd withdrawn. Anyway, I don't feel like I did the day before you arrived. I don't feel alone, I know some of my neighbors, I feel as if— as if I have value. As if I matter."

"You do matter." God, his chest was tightening with a mix of feelings he didn't even want to try to sort out.

"You helped me in more ways than you can possibly imagine, Ryder. When you leave, I'm going to build a life again. I'm not afraid of it anymore, just because you made me feel as if I'm not worthless. I'll never be able to thank you for that."

A smile began to stretch his face even as another icicle in his heart snapped and melted. "You helped me, too," he said when he could find voice. "You reminded me that I can actually make someone feel good."

"Oh, wow," she said, then rose from her seat and came around the table. He shoved back so that she could perch on his lap and he could wrap his arms around her.

"I'm kinda glad there was a tornado," he admitted before pressing his face to the warm, fragrant hollow between her neck and shoulder.

She lifted a hand to run her fingers through his hair. "Me, too. Just don't let the neighbors know."

He laughed and kissed her and suddenly wished like hell that he didn't have to go to Fresno. He'd made a promise, though, and he didn't break his promises. Besides, Ben was like a huge loose end hanging out there. Even if they never spoke again after his visit, it was important for both of them to clear the air. Brandy had loved her brother, and he owed it to her to give Ben as much peace of mind as he could.

But God, suicide was hard on the heart and mind. It created a whole extra layer of guilt and regret. Maybe less for Ben, because he hadn't been able to do much from across a continent, but it had sure scarred Ryder.

Thinking of those scars caused him to ease Marti off his lap, though he would have loved to keep her there. He had little enough to offer anyone right now, and although the time with her had gone a long way to making him feel better about himself, it hadn't cured the essential ill: Brandy was dead and now he could never answer the most basic question, had he done enough?

Maybe he would always wonder, but if so, he needed to find a way to make peace with that. Until he did, he had no business getting involved with another woman.

Even though he wanted to. Even though he was feeling an increasing desire to stay right here and try to put down some new roots. It wouldn't be fair to Marti, or to anyone, if he didn't get his head straightened out.

"Time to do the dishes," he said, as if it were the reason he had let her go. He couldn't bring himself to look at her. What if he saw something there, something that said he was hurting her or might hurt her?

He couldn't live with another victim on his soul.

The urge to clear out of here before he caused damage suddenly overwhelmed him. What the hell had he been thinking, making love to this woman and promising to do so again tonight?

He hadn't been thinking, he decided. He'd been needy and responding to those needs. Justifying it by thinking how needy she was didn't help much.

But then he remembered what she had said about how he'd helped change her self-image, making her feel more worthwhile, making her want to build a new life. She'd even mentioned his leaving.

So it was okay, he told himself, hoping he wasn't indulging in a bout of self-delusion. She'd thanked him and seemed to take it as inevitable that he wasn't going to stay.

Yes, it was okay. They were strangers helping each other through a stormy phase in their lives. Friendship, and certainly gratitude, might remain, but neither of those should cause either of them any grief.

As he dried dishes, he mentally ran through his list of the few things he was determined to finish before he left: the nursery, the last of the felled trees. A few days at most. Then he'd move on to Ben's and hopefully take care of the last of his demons.

It was almost as if running into Marti was some part of a grand design to reassure him that he could make a woman laugh and smile, that he could make a woman feel good.

So now that he knew that, he could face Ben's anger with more equanimity. More surety that he wasn't responsible for what happened to Brandy, although the question would never be undeniably answered.

One thing was for sure—he had found some unexpected healing here.

He'd been thinking about going out to the barn to work on the chair rails now that they had electricity, but he decided against it as he listened to the rain fall. He wasn't sure he'd be able to find an area large enough out there where water wouldn't be dripping through the roof.

Maybe, he thought, on his way back from Fresno he'd return here and fix a few more things. If she didn't mind.

But he didn't bring the subject up because it might be taken as a promise, and he wasn't at all sure how he was going to feel about things after his meeting with Ben.

Best not to leave any vague obligations behind him. It wouldn't be fair.

Not that he had a great belief in life's fairness, but he believed in it for himself.

Marti deserved better than that. A whole lot better.

Chapter 10

The rain had made a mess of the fields again. Disgusted, Ben spent the night in a town miles away from Conard City where he could at least stretch out on a bed. He found some businesses still open and bought an ugly brown dye for his sun-streaked hair, something that claimed he could do it himself at a sink. He also picked up some clothes that fit in better with the way people dressed around here. No cowboy boots, but he did buy the jeans and a checked Western shirt, even a cheap cowboy hat. He also finally ate a decent meal.

Okay, the endless hours of waiting had reinforced his decision not to kill the woman unless he had to. Knocking the karmic scales out of balance was seldom a smart thing. Unfortunately, he hadn't seen Ryder come out of the house once all day.

The idea that Ryder might be taking advantage of

another woman the way he'd taken advantage of Brandy began to grow in him. So it was Ben's job to save the Chastain woman, unless she got in his way or could tell the authorities who he was.

He liked the idea of being the woman's savior almost as much as he liked the idea of avenging Brandy. Well, if he could, he would, but vengeance was still on the top of his agenda.

However, he didn't have to be too uncomfortable while he pursued Ryder. He sprang for a small plastic tablecloth to put between him and the soggy ground and grass when he got to the field, and he picked up a couple of insulated bottles and had a drive-through attendant at fast-food joint fill them with hot coffee. He'd been missing his coffee, and those damn trail bars he'd bought were wearing thin as a diet.

When he at last headed back to the Chastain place before dawn, he was feeling really good about things. He still had today and tomorrow before he had to think about getting back. With any luck, he'd find some way to hide himself in that barn tonight and be ready for tomorrow.

Tomorrow was the day, he decided. It just felt right. Tomorrow or tomorrow night, depending on opportunity, unless something jumped right into his hands today. He whistled as he drove. Soon Brandy would truly rest.

Marti woke in the morning, stretching luxuriously, enjoying a few small kicks from Linda Marie that seemed almost like a greeting to her and the day. Last night had been filled with wonderful sex and that massage Ryder had promised, and she felt absolutely marvelous this morning.

But the bed was empty. She turned her head and found Ryder, fully clothed, looking out her window over the fields that were just becoming visible in the first rosy light of the day.

"Ryder? Is something wrong?"

He didn't stir for a minute. "No," he said finally. "You know how you felt watched a couple of times?"

Her heart quickened. She pushed herself up on her elbow. "Are you feeling it now?"

He shook his head. "No, not at all. It's something else."

"What?"

"I don't know. I just woke this morning with the feeling that something bad is going to happen."

"Do you get that feeling often?"

"Honestly, this is the first damn time. I have no reason at all for it, but it won't leave me alone."

She hesitated. "Then maybe you should pay attention to it."

He turned at last, giving her a crooked smile outlined by the rosy sky behind. "That's hard to justify."

"My mother used to say that if you had a bad feeling about something you should always listen to it. She said if nothing went wrong, fine. But if something did and you hadn't listened to the feeling you were going to be awfully sorry."

He came over and sat on the edge of the bed, and as he did so she could see his slight smile. "It'd be more helpful if I had some idea of what I thought might go wrong."

"True," she admitted. "But don't dismiss it. Maybe you'll get a feeling about something in particular later."

"Maybe." He bent over and kissed her long and deep. "Last night was heaven."

She thrilled to the words. "I thought so." Reaching up, she cupped his cheek, enjoying the scratchiness of his morning stubble.

"The thing is," he said bluntly, "that's what I want to be thinking about this morning, rather than some stupid feeling."

"Well," she said, looking at him from beneath her lashes, "you could always come back to bed."

A crack of laughter escaped him. "Don't tempt me. At least not until this feeling goes away. Let's go feed you something and then think about what we'll do today."

"Any ideas?"

His smile faded. "For starters, we're not doing anything that will leave you out of my sight."

"You think the feeling has to do with me?" Immediately her hands went to her stomach, but Linda Marie kicked reassuringly.

"I don't know. But if I'm going to take your mother's advice never to ignore such a feeling, it's all I can do. Unless it becomes more specific in some way."

He laid his hand over hers on her belly. "I think she's okay."

"She seems to be. Active. The doctor told me she'd become quieter toward the end, but right now she's busy."

"So let's go feed the little lady."

Not letting Marti out of his sight put a crimp on things he'd planned to do today, but the advice she had passed on from her mother made enough sense to him to stick to it.

He couldn't escape the crawling sensation of some impending doom, and although he wanted to dismiss it—if such feelings were useful, why hadn't he gotten that feeling the day he left for work only to come home and find Brandy dead?—it remained that it just made basic sense.

He couldn't shake the feeling. It hadn't just wafted across his mind like some stray nonsensical thought. It was clinging like damp, chilly leaves and he didn't like it.

Worse, he could think of a dozen ways things could go horribly wrong. He still got the willies watching Marti come down those steep stairs. She seemed to do it with the comfort of long familiarity, but he kept fearing she would over balance or miss a step, especially because she probably couldn't see the next step down. She had to be doing it by way of body memory.

So much in this house was rickety, too. What if a chair gave way? What if something happened while she was cooking? He was so damn glad they didn't have to rely on oil lamps anymore because every time he had put one down, part of him was waiting for something to shift and knock it over.

Although the house itself seemed sound and well-built, if in need of upkeep, nothing else was. What if a piece of linoleum lifted and she tripped on it?

A minor matter, unless you were pregnant.

Cripes, he told himself, just quit listing problems and keep an eye on the woman. Maybe the feeling would take care of itself.

But this meant he couldn't leave her to go work on the

chair railings in the barn. No way. He didn't want her out there in that moldy environment breathing spores and sawdust. Nor was he going to leave her inside to face the perils of stairs, linoleum and gas stoves while he went out to saw up the last of the trees.

He sighed as he helped her make breakfast and tried to plan a day that wouldn't leave them both feeling like caged tigers. She had so clearly enjoyed the painting yesterday that he wanted to get her involved in another fun activity. Hell, he'd taken pleasure in her enjoyment, too.

"Let's put the crib and changing table together this morning," he suggested. "Then maybe we can run to town. I'd like to pick up a few things."

The way her face lit up told him he'd hit on the right solution.

"But won't the furniture get in the way of you putting up the chair rails?" she asked.

"Nah. There's plenty of room in there to get it out of the way."

"Then let's do it," she said happily.

It made him feel good to have judged that one right. Of course she was eager to see the furniture set up, probably far more eager than she was to see the chair rails. It would occupy them cheerfully for a couple of hours before they went to town. And maybe when they left for town he'd be rid of this feeling.

It was weird how he couldn't ignore it. He wasn't used to this sort of thing and wondered if his brain had glitched somehow. Maybe it had been precipitated by her telling him that she had twice felt she was being watched.

That was a feeling he would never ignore. People had an uncanny sense of when eyes were on them, and he'd experienced it himself often only to be right. So maybe he'd built this feeling of something bad around the bend out of that.

Perhaps. It was the likeliest explanation he could think of, so he looked out every window before he settled into the nursery to start opening boxes and counting parts and pieces.

Apparently Marti wasn't worried about his feeling. She was smiling with excitement and oohing over every single piece.

"If you want, we can paint the crib with something safe for the baby," he said.

"I like the wood. Let's just leave it the way it is."

He liked it, too, and for a little while he was able to shove away the feeling as he worked with his hands. Of course, he would have built a better crib, but he didn't say so. Instead he focused his efforts on making it as sturdy as he could as they assembled it.

This was good enough and he still had promises to keep.

Ben grew increasingly annoyed. Neither one of them emerged from the house all morning. When they finally did, it was early afternoon, and they climbed into the pickup truck and drove away.

He rolled over on his back and considered. He'd already planned his move for tomorrow. He felt good about tomorrow, although he couldn't say why. Yet he may have just been handed the only opportunity he'd have to get close to that house and barn and get inside. What if neither of them stepped outside tomorrow?

He had no idea of the lay of the land over there. Ryder

seemed to be showing very little interest in spending time in the barn.

Maybe the best thing would be to attack inside the house. It would involve the woman, but with his hair dyed and his face unshaven for several days, he doubted she'd be able to give a good description of him. He looked down at himself, at the new clothes that were already beginning to look soiled from crawling around out here, and decided he was beginning to look like some kind of drifter.

Good.

Because he no longer had to conceal himself from Ryder and the Chastain woman, he stood up and walked back to the road. The best thing to do would be to scope out the house and barn. Find a place to conceal himself. Figure out how to carry out the attack. Time was getting short. If he didn't get back to Fresno soon, he'd run out of vacation time and someone would notice. He couldn't afford to have anyone notice anything about him.

He just wished he knew how long the two of them were going to be gone. It'd be far easier to drive up to the house than walk. But as soon as he thought that, he shook his head at his own stupidity. He was going up there to kill. He wasn't coming back out until he was done with Ryder.

So he turned and walked to the end of the woman's driveway and hiked toward the house. He had all he needed—some coffee in a thermos, a penlight and his knife. His very sharp knife, carefully chosen for this task.

And as soon as he could, he was going to use it.

Driving away from the farm dissipated the uneasiness that had been plaguing Ryder since first awakening. It didn't entirely vanish, but it stopped nagging at him so much. Hoping it was gone for good, not all that eager to test it, he kept them in town doing every possible thing he could think of.

He took Marti window shopping at Freitag's but was careful not to buy any of the stuff she seemed to like. He was well aware that she was already uncomfortable with how much he'd done, and he didn't want to make her uncomfortable today. Besides, he figured if he started picking up things that she liked, she'd stop looking. So he enjoyed her pleasure and made mental notes in case the future ever brought him an opportunity to do something about it.

Since he had a cell connection again, he called Ben but got no answer. He left a message saying he'd be here only a few more days.

It bothered him to think of leaving Marti, but he had to keep his promise to visit Ben. Maybe after all that was done he'd be settled enough in his own mind and heart to know what he wanted to do next. He thought that might involve Marti, but how could he be sure? Fond as he was growing of that woman, he wasn't sure enough of how he felt about himself to know what he had to offer anyone else.

Besides, it would be good for him to get away for a little while. He wasn't sure that he wasn't living in some fantasy universe at the moment, living out some kind of dream where he could do the kind of thing he liked best with a beautiful woman at his side and a baby on the way.

It wasn't even his baby, but he felt a growing attachment to Linda Marie, envisioning how it would be when she was born, what it would be like to hold her and hear her coos and giggles. Was it normal for a man to feel that way for a baby that wasn't his and hadn't even been born yet? How the hell would he know?

But he needed to get away, to make sure his head was clear and not fogged over by some illusion that filled a lot of the gaps in his life.

When Marti started to tire, he took her around the corner to the City Diner for beverages and a snack. The service at the place wasn't great, given that the large woman who evidently owned the place slammed things down and stomped around as if she were perpetually angry.

"She always does that," Marti whispered. "It's just her manner."

Her food made up for it, he supposed, because even at mid-afternoon, the place was busy.

When she brought them an appetizer of battered mushrooms, she regarded Ryder with a basilisk eye. "You that guy Micah mentioned?"

"Ryder," he said.

"You best be taking good care of that little lady."

"He is," Marti answered swiftly. "He's helping me a lot, Maude."

"Hmm." Maude gave him another glare and stomped away.

Ryder arched a brow at Marti. "Was that a pass or fail?"

She giggled. "Don't ask me. I'm still new to these parts."

Not as new as she thought, he decided as he helped himself to a mushroom. Whether she knew it or not, this community seemed to have begun to wrap itself around

Marti. He decided that before he left, he'd ask Micah and Ransom to keep an eye on her. He was sure they would.

That made him feel a bit better. Just a bit.

After Marti felt refreshed, she suggested the bookstore. There he broke his rule, and when he saw her look longingly at a couple of novels, he insisted on buying them. He also bought a pack of cards and challenged her to a game that evening.

"I haven't played cards much," she admitted. "Have you?"

"Used to do it all the time on lunch breaks at work sites. I'm going to kill you."

That elicited another of her glorious laughs.

He dragged the day out as long as he could, with a stop at the hardware store for some finishing nails he'd forgotten, with dinner at Maude's so Marti wouldn't have to cook.

The way he dragged it out began to get through to him. Was he worried about returning to her place because of that feeling he'd had earlier? Or was he simply drawing out the pleasant day because each passing minute was bringing him closer to his departure?

Neither idea made him happy. But finally, when he looked at Marti, he couldn't escape the inevitable. She was getting tired. She needed to put her feet up.

Enough of his self-indulgence. Regardless of its source, he was being thoughtless.

Time to head home and to whatever awaited. He just wished the feeling was a good one.

It was a good day for Ben. He searched the barn and the house to make sure he knew where everything was. He found some rope, which he could use to tie the woman up so she couldn't call for help after he took care of Ryder, giving him plenty of time to get away.

He found the phone line and cut it, then twisted it back together so it wouldn't show. No help would come for a long time, not until that woman could get free and get to her truck. Long enough for his escape.

He discarded the idea of hiding in the barn. Ryder might not show up there until some time tomorrow. But he would come into the house and getting into the house, by way of the backdoor proved easy. Lousy locks, maybe because folks around here didn't get afraid. He was going to change that tonight.

He explored the house carefully and discovered that the upstairs hall floorboards creaked beneath his feet. Definitely not good, but he couldn't imagine a plan of going for Ryder while he was awake and downstairs. That would risk too much in this tiny house.

He considered the barn again, but Ryder hadn't been out there in two days now. Time was running out.

So he paced the hallway until he realized that if he kept very close to the wall, the boards didn't creak at all. He practiced it a few times to be sure he had it memorized.

Then he explored the rooms. One clearly appeared to be where Ryder was staying. His duffel, jacket and clothes were there. At the other end of the hall was the woman's room, identified by the paltry selection of clothing in her closet. But then he saw something that made him freeze with anger.

A pair of men's jeans lay over the back of a rickety chair. Damn it, Ryder was sleeping with her.

For a time his vision turned so red he thought the

fury was going to burst out of him. It was all he could do to keep from smashing something.

Steadily he forced himself back to an icy calm. Tonight Ryder would pay for all his sins. Tonight. The promise soothed him.

The nursery, smelling of fresh paint, seemed the best place to hide. There was a closet that held nothing and the door hinges didn't even squeak. No reason for anyone to go into it. It was midway between the two bedrooms so it wouldn't matter where Ryder slept tonight. He'd have easy access to either end of the hall.

What's more, Ryder and the Chastain woman could glance into the open nursery and it would never occur to them to look any farther. He also had a view of the driveway, so he waited until he saw the truck coming. Then he settled into the closet with his knife, his penlight, his energy bars and his thermos refilled with water. He left the door open just a crack so that he could see anyone who came in here.

Soon, he thought with satisfaction. Soon. All he had to do was sneak up on Ryder while they were sleeping. If the woman woke, she wouldn't be able to do much when faced with a knife. He'd be able to tie her up while Ryder bled to death.

Then he'd have all the time in the world.

Dusk had fallen by the time Marti and Ryder returned to the farmhouse. Marti was weary, so Ryder suggested she put her feet up while he got them something to drink and set up the card table so they could play.

As he got them tall glasses of orange juice and put together a plate of crackers in case her stomach decided to turn queasy, Ryder paused.

Staring out through the window over the sink, he had the oddest feeling that he'd found what he never had. He wasn't quite sure what it was. These cozy, comfortable evenings? The quiet life of labor? The fresh new nights of love?

Everything was so laid back and comfortable with Marti. He enjoyed her company. He enjoyed the quiet times with her in the evening as much as he enjoyed working around this place. Maybe more.

He tried to remind himself that it was all fresh and new, that he hadn't been here long, that he had no long-term metric. But this was all so different from the way it had been with Brandy, maybe he was just succumbing to an illusion of peace and warmth that was ephemeral.

Of course it was ephemeral. He had to get on to Fresno soon. Only then would he be in a position to decide whether he really wanted to come back here.

Maybe he was just hiding out in this cocoon in order to feel better for a while before returning to the reality of his life. Before facing Ben and dealing once again with the tragedy and pain of Brandy.

He stifled a sigh, hating that he wasn't really sure of himself. He'd always been certain of what he was thinking and feeling, but now he wondered. It would be too easy to take a stab at refuge right now. To hide out and pretend the rest of the world didn't exist.

Was that what he was doing?

He supposed it was possible. He'd been busy shucking every reminder of his old life. Maybe he just wanted a new one ready-made without all the hassle of making it.

But then he thought of Marti in his arms and knew one thing for certain. He wanted her. Making love with her had been among the very best experiences of his life. He even had grown fond of that baby bump.

Okay, so maybe he had some business here to think about later. After Fresno. After he'd taken whatever shellacking Ben doled out and did his best to explain the unexplainable.

Because even while he had lived with it for years, there was no real way he could understand the pain that had finally made Brandy think death would be better than life. He figured no one who hadn't been there would ever understand.

But he'd also been trying for eight months to live with it, and it didn't seem to be getting easier. He wondered if thoughts of failure would dog him the rest of his days.

Marti had eased a bit of that. She'd made him feel like it was possible for him to make a woman happier if not happy. For that he would always be grateful to her.

But she deserved more than gratitude, he didn't want to leave and the whole thing is his mind was getting a little mixed up. What exactly did he feel for Marti?

Going to Fresno, getting away for a week, might make that considerably clearer, he decided. It only remained to find out if she wanted to see him on his way back from California.

If she did, then he'd be free of his last obligation to Brandy and maybe better able to sort it all out. If she didn't... Well, he'd deal with that.

But he was growing increasingly certain that he was going to leave at least a small piece of his withered heart behind him in Wyoming.

Marti was tired from their day in town, but it was a good tired, the kind that had come from having a lot of fun.

She couldn't remember this place ever having felt so much like a home as it did now with the card table adjusted so that she could play with her feet up and Ryder facing her across it with a grin, teasing her mercilessly about her total lack of knowledge when it came to card games.

"You do know what a card looks like, don't you?" he asked, holding up the deck.

"Of course!"

"Now what about suits and the value of each card?"

She giggled. "I'm not that dumb. I just haven't played that much. Not since I was in high school, and even then I didn't play often."

"Ah, a neophyte for the plucking."

"There isn't much to pluck."

"Points," he said. "You'd better hope you have a great case of beginner's luck."

"I'm the world's luckiest beginner," she joked.

It got even funnier when he spent the first few rounds playing her hand for her to explain what was going on. She had no idea what the game was, didn't even care, but she got a big kick out of him rounding the table to perch on the arm of her chair, pick up her cards and say, "Now, what would Marti do?"

If he still felt that uneasiness from this morning, he hadn't mentioned it all day. For that she was grateful. She tried not to be superstitious at all, but the simple fact was she had been raised by a very superstitious mother. There were some things she couldn't quite shake to this day.

But Ryder seemed fine now and kept her laughing and smiling until her eyelids grew too heavy to hold up any longer.

She must have dozed off because all of a sudden there was a gentle hand on her shoulder, shaking her.

"Come on, let's get you to bed," Ryder said.

She yawned and blinked herself back to some kind of awareness. He helped her rise to her feet and followed her up the stairs as if he were afraid she might fall. His big hands rested lightly on her hips, ready to steady her.

"Did you ever play train when you were a kid?" she asked sleepily.

"You mean like this?" His hands pushed gently, alternating between her hips as he made a choo-choo sound.

A giggle started to emerge but a yawn grabbed her instead. He was right behind her every step of the way to her bedroom, and she offered no objection as he helped her undress.

Why would she? she thought as he sat her on the side of the bed and lifted away her clothing one bit at a time, kissing her flesh as he exposed it.

"You're waking me up," she pretended to grouse.

"Not much, and I'm not going to keep you awake. Not tonight. Anyone who dozes off like you just did needs sleep."

"But…"

He silenced her with a kiss. "I'll take a raincheck for the morning."

"Promise?"

"Promise."

The warm fires that had started to grow deep inside her settled down, feeling nice but not demanding. He pulled her nightshirt over her head, then tucked her in like a baby.

"Sweet dreams," he said. "I'm going to read for a while. I'll be up later."

She wanted to protest his departure, didn't want to lose a single minute with him, but had to admit that she really was too tired. Turning over on her side, sleep crept up on her even as she heard his footsteps go down the hall and down the stairs.

He'd said he'd come back later. She sighed and drifted away.

Chapter 11

In the nursery, Ben was about ready to blow a gasket. The woman was upstairs, he'd heard Ryder go back downstairs and now he couldn't do a damn thing. No way would he get downstairs without alerting Ryder to his presence.

Cramped in the closet, he was growing very uncomfortable and cussed under his breath as he wondered how long it would be. An hour? More? And then he'd have to give Ryder time to fall asleep, too.

Crap, this hadn't been his wisest choice in this whole business, but he still couldn't think of a better way.

Maybe Ryder wasn't sleeping with the woman after all, but it didn't change Ben's feelings any. He'd heard the two of them laughing, and it had kept his anger at a full simmer for the past couple of hours.

Ryder laughing. With his wife not in the ground a whole year. Major burn.

He fingered the knife he held, testing its razor-sharp edge with his thumb. Patience, he counseled himself. He'd waited this long, and sooner or later Ryder would return upstairs, and because of that creaking hallway, the house would tell him which room Ryder went to.

He kind of cherished the hope that Ryder would head away from the woman. He'd really rather not have her involved. He didn't directly blame her for Ryder's sins, and it would be so much easier and safer to only have to deal with one of them.

Peering out the crack he'd left open in the closet door, he waited and listened. If there was one thing his abbreviated time in the army had taught him, it was that he was capable of dealing with a whole lot, and Ryder and that pregnant woman weren't as big a problem as some he'd dealt with.

Counting his breaths, he drew relaxation over himself like a cloak. The time would come when he'd need his anger and adrenaline, but it would be stupid to get worn out from it in advance.

Relax. The situation was fluid but still under his control. Most definitely.

Ryder couldn't quite settle. Although he hadn't mentioned it to Marti again, he still had that uneasy sense that something bad was going to happen. He prowled downstairs, checking every window and door to be sure they were locked. He ought to hear if anyone tried to get in.

At last he sat down to read a book, but couldn't relax into it. With each word he read, he was aware that his senses were hyperacute, listening for any sound that wasn't ordinary.

He tried to talk himself down. After all, he'd seen exactly nothing to heighten his concern and Marti's feeling of being watched a couple of times could have been some animal. After the tornado, only God knew what might have been displaced and was looking for a new home. He was willing to bet this area had mountain lions, and Marti had even once mentioned wolves in the mountains. Man, it could have even been a neighbor's dog that had gotten through a destroyed fence.

After a few hours, he heard Marti climb out of bed, and he could hear her light step in the hallway going toward the bathroom. He smiled faintly. He'd gotten used to her frequent needs that could drag her out of bed several times a night and that had made her say earlier today that she needed to be within dashing distance of a bathroom at all times.

She had joked about it, but he spent some minutes wondering just how much of an effect a pregnancy had on so much. Adding twenty to twenty-five pounds all in one place…well, things were going to get moved around or squished. One of the things he liked about her was that she never complained about it. He wondered if he would be so positive if he were the one bearing the load.

But she really wanted this baby. He hoped he got to see Linda Marie after she was born. The tug toward the whole notion of that little girl's birth had been growing in him from the start, from the first kick. Maybe he was stupid, but he hadn't thought a man would feel such a thing for another man's unborn child.

But there it was, making his reluctance to move on all the greater. He didn't need that, he warned himself. He had to go see Ben. Only then could he decide what to do after.

Marti's footsteps emerged from the bathroom, then paused. He smiled to himself, thinking she had stopped to admire the nursery. She had been doing that ever since they had painted and papered it, and now there was furniture, too.

If he never gave her anything else, at least he'd given her part of her dream. That settled warmly in his heart, melting the last of the ice he'd been carrying for so long.

He was capable of taking care of a woman. He was capable of making one smile and laugh.

God knew, he'd spent years wondering if he ever could or would.

Ben had had enough. Hours were ticking away and he had to take care of this tonight. He couldn't sit here forever, and what if someone came by in the early morning? No, this had to be done now.

The woman going to the bathroom suddenly struck him as an opportunity. He eased out of the closet and slid his way slowly to the nursery door, covered by the sounds of running water. Then he waited.

When the Chastain woman emerged, paused at the nursery, and the door started to open, he knew his moment had come. He grabbed her the instant the door opened and she stood frozen in shock. Shock helped him. It made him possible for him to seize her, whip her around and hold her tight with one arm beneath her breasts and the knife at her throat.

Then she helped him by letting out a shriek. In moments Ryder would come running.

"Shut up or I'll cut your throat," he said to the woman. She immediately fell silent and still. "I don't want to hurt you. I want Ryder."

He felt her tense then relax again. Docile. Exactly what he wanted her to be. And he had no doubt that with his training he would be able to overpower Ryder and take him out. With a little help from the woman, of course.

Yes, she would be helpful.

He heard the stampede of Ryder's booted feet on the staircase. Moments later, his enemy filled the doorway, looking stunned.

"Don't say anything," he barked at Ryder. "Does she know who I am?"

Ryder's hands clenched and unclenched. "Why would she?" he said. "Damn, I told you, I'm just working around here."

"You seem a little cozy, the two of you. Maybe I should just cut her now."

"What good would that do?" Ryder demanded. "It's me you want, right?"

"You better believe it. You killed your wife."

Ryder froze. "Maybe I did," he said finally.

It was music to Ben's ears. "So the question is," he said, "whether I'm going to just take you out, or take her out, too."

Smiling, he waited, enjoying having the upper hand.

Ryder rode the edge of panic. Not for himself. He didn't care what happened to him, but the sight of Ben with a knife to Marti's throat almost overcame him. There were two lives he had to protect no matter the cost.

He forced himself to focus, to shove the panic back. To find out what Ben wanted so maybe he could gain some control here.

"Is it just me you want?" he asked. "Because if so, you can put her aside right now and deal with me."

"No," Ben said. "That would be too easy for you. If I thought you'd give enough of a damn if I killed this woman, I'd do it just to see you hurt the way you didn't hurt when Brandy died."

"I didn't hurt?" The idea stunned Ryder. "I hurt like hell."

"Right. But you killed her. So you're going to pay. And maybe this woman will be part of the price. One slit and she's gone, Ryder, and then I can take care of you."

One slit and she'd be gone, all right. Of that Ryder had not the least doubt. In that instant he realized he had to convince Ben he didn't give a damn about Marti, that he was some kind of cold-blooded ass who hadn't cared about his wife and didn't care about this woman.

"What," he asked quietly, "makes you think I give any more of a damn about this woman than I did about Brandy? I just met her. I stopped to do some carpentry work, that's all. There was a freaking hole in her roof, she's a nice lady, so I helped. But you think I give a damn about someone else's pregnant bitch?" He heard her gasp, but he couldn't bring himself to look at Marti as he spoke those words. They felt like knives in his own heart, and he could only think they struck Marti just the same. Nor could he afford to think about that now.

Ben's smile was growing. "I knew you were heartless. You use women. Was she the next you were going to kick away?"

"We hadn't even gotten that far. I was leaving and she knew it. What kind of woman do you take her for?"

"One who could fall sway to your charms the way Brandy did."

"Well, she didn't. Too bad you didn't wait. I was leaving tomorrow."

Marti was visibly sagging. Ben's expression was changing to one of great satisfaction.

"Look," Ryder said, "take it out on me. Why make such a big mess the cops will never stop looking for you? Lock her in her bedroom and deal with me."

Ben paused to consider. "How can I lock her in? Doors lock from the inside."

"This is an old house. The doors can be locked from the outside with a key. Just put her in there. Make her promise to stay until you're gone."

Ben hesitated. "Do you think Ryder cares about you?" he asked Marti.

Ryder almost flinched when he saw the deadness of her expression, the paleness of her face.

"No," she whispered. "He never did."

The words dropped into Ryder's heart like knives as sharp as the one Ben was holding. She meant them. He could hear the truth in them. But he fought down the overwhelming pain. What happened to him didn't matter. Only what happened to Marti.

"Come on," he managed to say. "She doesn't matter to me, and she sure as hell doesn't matter to you. So just lock her up and let's have it out."

Ben spoke to Marti. "You got a key so I can lock you in?"

"Yes," she whispered.

He returned his attention to Ryder. "Then go out back and wait for me. I don't want you looking over my shoulder while I lock her up."

"I can help."

"I don't trust you. Get the hell out before I slit her

throat! Make sure you wait for me, or I will come back up here and cut her to ribbons and it'll be on your head, like Brandy."

So Ryder turned and walked away from the woman he only now realized had become the most precious thing in his life. With every step, dread grew. What if Ben didn't just lock her up?

But he could see no other way. If he attacked Ben, it might only get Marti killed or hurt.

So he headed out back. Along the way he grabbed Marti's biggest butcher knife and concealed it under his shirt.

Please, God, he prayed harder than he had prayed for anything since Brandy's death, save her. Don't let Ben hurt her.

Ben urged Marti down the hall to her bedroom at knifepoint. She put up no fuss. The baby, she reminded herself. Damn Ryder to hell, but she had to save the baby. Thoughts of Linda Marie kept her docile, led her to her dresser to pull out one of the big old-fashioned keys to the room and hand it to the guy. Ben, she supposed, though she wouldn't give away that she had guessed.

She didn't tell him there was a second key at the back of the drawer, that she had no intention of remaining indefinitely locked in this room once this was over. Plus, once she unlocked the door from the inside and relocked it from the inside, as long as she left the key in the lock, no one would be able to open the door from the outside.

That man was not going to get back in here, nor was she going to be locked up any longer than she chose.

"You stay and be a good girl," Ben said to her. "I really don't want to kill you. Too much karma."

He was thinking about murdering Ryder, but killing her was too much karma? Her mind whirled with the craziness of his thinking—and with the shock of the things Ryder had said.

If only she hadn't believed him when he said he didn't care about another man's pregnant bitch.

Much to her relief, Ben locked her in. She waited until she heard him start down the stairs, then she hurried to unlock the door. Thank God he hadn't left the key in the keyhole. She unlocked it and then relocked it from the inside, leaving the key in place.

She could get out now.

Her first thought was to call the sheriff, but when she picked up the phone beside her bed, she got a dead line.

Slowly she sat on the bed as her heart ached, her mind whirled and she tried to deal with both anguish and terror.

Maybe Ryder didn't give a damn about her. But she gave a damn about him. Was she just going to sit here while he was killed?

Anger at what he had said burst in her like a dam. But the bottom line was not what kind of man Ryder was. No, it was what kind of woman she was.

Her thoughts turned to the shotgun on the closet shelf behind a stack of old sweatshirts.

She fought back the anger and pain and made herself start thinking.

Ryder stepped out in the backyard of the house so he'd be in a puddle of darkness if Ben turned on lights. It would be the only advantage he'd have. Ben had bragged often enough about his tour in the army, truncated though it had been according to Brandy.

He was up against a formidable enemy, one who had skills he had never had to learn. He thought of the look on Marti's face when he'd said those ugly words, and he figured it didn't matter if he died. He'd just tossed away the only good thing he'd known in years.

He pulled the knife from beneath his shirt and laid it flat against his right thigh, making sure that his side was to the house so Ben wouldn't see it. God, what had gotten into the man? He had never dreamed Ben's anger had grown to this extreme. But what bothered him even more was the way Ben seemed to be enjoying this. It was sick beyond belief.

Then he heard the screen door screech and looked. Ben flicked on the kitchen light just as he was emerging.

The one thing Ryder wanted to know was whether Marti was okay. But he didn't dare ask, for fear of letting Ben know that he did care.

"I'm here," was all he said.

"I see you." But switching on the light had given Ryder, who stood in the darkness, the smallest of temporary advantages. It would take at least a few moments for Ben to readapt to the dark. Small blessings.

Ben loped easily toward him, knife ready. Ryder waited until the last second before raising his own knife. Ben stopped immediately.

"Well, well," he said. "I see you want a fight. You don't know what to do with that knife."

"Maybe not, but I'm not going like an animal to slaughter."

"So much the better. I'll enjoy it more, cutting you before I kill you."

Ryder braced himself. This was going to hurt, it was

going to be tough, and all he could think about was Marti.

Focus! The order sounded loud inside his own head, though it never escaped his mouth. He felt his vision widening, taking in everything about Ben, not just his knife.

To the death, he thought. Never had he wanted anything to come to this.

Ben launched himself, and almost before Ryder realized it, he felt a stinging in his upper arm that told him he'd been cut.

In that instant, thought fled. Survival instincts took over and they were good ones.

He whirled around, returning the cut as Ben came at him again. With his other arm he swung upward at Ben's jaw at the same instant.

There was something to be said for having been in a few bar brawls in his youth.

Ben stumbled and Ryder dropped his knife, choosing to dive at Ben and bring him to the ground.

That was where he came up against the fact that Ben worked out at a gym. Ben had more power. Trying to pin his arms and especially that knife to the ground was like trying to move a ten-ton boulder with one hand. Again and again he just barely managed to deflect.

Ben gave a twist of his lower body and Ryder helplessly rolled. Suddenly Ben was above him, and that knife was dangerously close.

He grabbed Ben's wrist again and held the weapon away. That was when he felt his first stirring of hope. Ben's power was greater, but because of the way he'd built that strength, he didn't have the endurance that Ryder had gained through long days of hard work. He could feel the faintest of tremors begin in the arm he struggled against.

Sensing a real hope of victory, he pushed as hard as he could, rolling and slamming Ben's knife hand to the ground.

The knife skittered away as he rose up to straddle Ben's chest, locking him in place.

Now what? Ryder wondered. He glanced toward the knife and debated whether to grab it, realizing that he might only lose control of it and re-arm Ben.

Rearing back a little, he punched Ben in the jaw again.

Then a sound froze them both.

It was the unmistakable sound of a shotgun being pumped.

Marti stood on her back porch, shotgun aimed at both of them. Her knees felt almost weak, but only determination kept her going.

"I'm a fair shot," she said. "You two break it up now or I'll shoot you both."

Ryder, still straddling Ben, said, "Can I at least get rid of the knives? I don't want him grabbing one."

Marti hesitated, wondering what the hell she was going to do next. She wondered how long she could keep control of Ben. Regardless of what he'd said, though, she trusted Ryder and didn't at all trust Ben.

"Go ahead," she said coldly. "This thing is loaded with double-aught. It'll get both of you if one of you does anything stupid."

Ryder looked down at Ben, who was bleeding from his mouth. "She will shoot. Don't try anything."

Ben hardly mumbled.

Ryder rose and kicked both knives away as far as he could send them. Ben was struggling to sit up, but Ryder pushed him back down. He looked at Marti. "I need to tie him up. Can I go to the barn? Can you keep that gun on him?"

"If he moves a muscle he's gone. He threatened my baby."

That, thought Ryder as he limped toward the barn, heedless of the blood running down his arm, wondering why the hell his leg ached, was the bottom line. Ben had threatened her baby.

The mama bear was furious.

Ben made the mistake of trying to get to his feet. Marti pointed the shotgun a safe distance away and fired it. Then she pumped it again. "Next time it's your head."

Ben slumped back to the ground.

Ryder came tearing back with rope and froze as he took in the scene. "Thank God," was all he said. He immediately went to work hog-tying Ben as tightly as he could.

Then he sat back on his heels and looked up at Marti. "Now what? We need help. We can't sit on this guy forever."

"I know. The cops are coming. The idiot cut a phone line, but it was the line to my bedroom. He didn't get the line to the kitchen phone."

"How is that possible?"

"It's an old house. We installed the second line in the bedroom and they put in separate wiring."

"Thank God," Ryder said again. "Do you trust me to take over shotgun duty?"

She hesitated visibly, thinking about the things he had

said. But one thing she knew for sure: Ryder had painted her nursery, helped her in countless ways and had never threatened her, whatever else he might think about her.

"Do you know how to use it?"

"Yes."

"Okay." Because she suddenly felt a strong need to collapse. As soon as she turned over the gun to Ryder, she went inside, tumbled onto the living room chair and began to cry her eyes out.

The words he had spoken had pierced her heart like acacia thorns. She wondered if the pain would ever go away.

Chapter 12

Cops and EMTs arrived. Ben was arrested, and the EMTs checked Marti out and then bandaged Ryder's arm. The swirl of cops lasted a couple of hours as they gathered evidence and took statements.

Dawn still hadn't arrived when they finally departed and the house fell silent again. Ryder hesitated just inside the living room, looking at Marti, his heart squeezing almost violently with the pain he felt. Her face had gone dead and was still streaked with dried tears. He had wounded her, he knew it, and he wondered if he would ever be able to get around it.

"You need to sleep," he said finally.

"I need you to leave."

"I will. In the morning. After we talk."

"I don't want to talk to you."

He didn't argue. He simply took the afghan that hung over the back of another chair and spread it over her.

"Sleep," he said. "I'll be gone as soon as I've had my say. But later."

The way she looked at him should have killed him. Instead it made him head for the kitchen where he'd be out of sight. He made a pot of coffee and sat down, planning to remain awake.

It was time to get his head straightened out, no matter how much pain it caused him, and he needed to do it fast.

Marti slept from exhaustion. Upset and hurt as she was, she couldn't fight sleep forever. Her dreams were troubled and scary for the first time in forever, but she slept deeply mostly because her pregnancy demanded it.

When she awoke, the sun was high and her body ached all over. Probably all the tension she thought because she hadn't been hurt.

Last night crashed home vividly, the anguish so deep and painful she thought it would rip her in two.

Ryder, who had been so kind to her all this time, had said such an awful thing that she wondered if he were as twisted as Ben. How could he be so nice and then so cruel? Maybe he had been partly responsible for his wife's death. If he made a habit of saying such things, she could well believe it possible.

But even though she had heard the words with her own ears, she didn't want to believe them. But how could she not believe them? It sounded so much like a man not to want any part of another man's child. Hell, her baby's own father hadn't been especially interested.

Why should Ryder care at all?

No, he didn't care, and she shouldn't have allowed herself to be deluded by the kindness he'd shown. Maybe he was essentially a kind man, but he'd always made it clear he was leaving.

She was the one who had fallen head-first into a fantasy of her own making. He had never promised one damn thing. After all, she was pregnant with another man's child.

"Marti?" Ryder's voice was tentative.

She looked toward the entry to the living room, and even as her heart felt as if it were sundering, she couldn't help but eat him up with her eyes. He was a glorious figure of a man, and just the sight of him reminded her of their lovemaking, reminded her she wanted more of it, more of him.

But not if he could say things like that.

"I told you to leave."

"I said I'd go after we talked. I'm all packed."

Surprisingly those words caused another shaft of pain, but she tried not to let it show.

"I have some crackers for you. Do you feel comfortable enough for coffee or milk?"

She didn't feel at all nauseated. "Coffee," she said finally, reluctantly. Her brain felt as fried as the rest of her, and she figured she needed some caffeine to get through this hellacious morning.

Ryder set the plate of crackers on her lap and a mug of coffee on the table beside her. Ignoring him, she ate a couple of crackers then sipped coffee. Her stomach remained content. It was the only part of her that seemed to be.

Ryder then surprised her by kneeling beside her chair. Part of her wanted to reach out to him, but another part wanted to recoil. She froze.

"The things I said last night to Ben," he began, "they

weren't true. Not that I killed my wife, not that you didn't matter to me."

"Right. Another man's pregnant bitch. That just came out of nowhere."

"It came out of my desire to convince Ben I didn't care about you because I was afraid of what he'd do if he thought he could hurt me by hurting you. I didn't mean one word of it."

"You walked away and left me alone with him."

"What was I supposed to do? Attack him? He had a knife at your throat. You'd have been dead before I reached him."

"And he could have killed me after you walked away."

"I know," he said simply. "I was scared to death, but I couldn't see any other way of drawing him away from you. I was the one he really wanted. You didn't matter to him at all if you weren't a way to hurt me. But I was terrified. Walking away from you was the hardest thing I've ever done. Ever. But I wanted you safely away in your bedroom. I knew you could lock it so he couldn't get back to you. I thought you could call the cops."

She thought it over and hated to feel some of the pain lessening, if only a tiny bit. "You were leaving anyway," she said finally. "It doesn't matter. Just go."

"It matters to me!" He said the words forcefully. "Damn it, Marti, this time with you hasn't been a sham. I'm sorry my head's been so mixed up, but the bottom line was that the only, absolutely only, reason I was going to leave was because I had a promise to keep. And I didn't want to go. I didn't want to go at all. But I couldn't tell you that until after I got the mess in my head sorted out because you matter too damn much to me to make you promises unless I can keep them. Unless I've figured out things enough to be sure of who I am."

Her heart lifted a little and she tried to tamp down a rising hope. Hope could only mean pain. "Are you ever going to get your head sorted out?"

"I did. Last night was remarkably clarifying."

"Meaning?"

"That I would have died to save you. That the only thing I was worried about last night was you and Linda Marie. You want to talk about clear? Last night was a damn epiphany. I didn't care what that madman did to me as long as you were safe."

The little bubble that was trying to lift her heart lifted it a bit higher. "Honestly?"

"Honestly. I realized that if anything happened to you I might as well be dead. And you want to know something? I didn't come close to what I felt last night when I lost Brandy. With Brandy, as much as it hurt, there was almost an inevitability to it, as if I'd been losing her for years and knew that at some point I wasn't going to be able to hang on to her forever. With you...I couldn't have stood it. I simply could not have survived it."

He reached for her hand and she let him. Inside she felt the hurt beginning to ease.

"Marti, you taught me how to live again. How to laugh again. You taught me I could make a woman happy, at least in little ways. You made me feel good about myself. Do you know how long it's been since I felt good about myself? Years. I've been feeling like an utter failure since Brandy's sickness took over. Every day was a survival strategy. I couldn't even get her to smile most of the time. But you've made me feel it wasn't me. I wasn't her problem. You did a better job of that than all the shrinks we saw."

"I don't want you hanging out with me because of gratitude," she said slowly.

"Gratitude! That's the least of it. Lady, I'm trying to say that I love you, heart, body and soul, and I don't ever want to be away from you. I want to stay right here and love you and Linda Marie for the rest of my days. I just hope I've been half as good for you as you've been for me."

Her heart began to feel as light as a balloon. "You really don't mind another man's kid?"

"If you let me, Linda Marie will be mine. She was at the top of my fears last night. You and she were all I cared about and I'd have cut my own throat to protect you."

She didn't have to think about it long. She remembered every single one of the ways he had cared for her and the baby and held it up to statements made in an attempt to prevent a lunatic from hurting her and decided which she believed in.

"I didn't want you to leave, either," she admitted. "But you were so determined to go, and I tried not to get deeply involved with you but…"

His eyes had begun to shine. "But what?"

"You really, really want the baby, too?"

"You can put my name on the birth certificate if you want. As far as I'm concerned, you two are a package and I want you both. Forever."

She lifted her arms to him then and he leaned over her, kissing her with gentle passion, laying his hand on her belly as if to cradle the baby, too.

"I love you," he murmured against her lips. "God,

I never thought I'd love anyone again, and I never dreamed I could love this much."

"I love you, too," she answered, admitting it at last to both herself and him. "Don't ever leave me."

"Never. I'll be here when we're both old and gray."

Her heart took flight at last, joy filled her until happy tears rolled down her cheeks. What had begun with a near catastrophe had almost ended with another catastrophe, but now they had led her straight to the place she most wanted to be on earth.

In Ryder's protective arms.

* * * * *

COMING NEXT MONTH from Harlequin
Romantic Suspense®
AVAILABLE JUNE 19, 2012

#1711 HER COWBOY DISTRACTION
Cowboy Café
Carla Cassidy
When Lizzy Wiles blew into town, she never expected a handsome cowboy to capture her interest...or that someone wanted her dead.

#1712 IN THE ENEMY'S ARMS
Marilyn Pappano
As a humanitarian trip to Cozumel turns deadly, there's only one person Cate Calloway can turn to: her longtime enemy Justin Seavers.

#1713 AT HIS COMMAND
To Protect and Serve
Karen Anders
Lieutenant Commander Sia Soto is on a collision course with danger. Only the sexy man she left behind can get her out alive.

#1714 UNDERCOVER SOLDIER
Linda O. Johnston
Sherra Alexander is shocked when her purportedly dead high school sweetheart appears in her apartment—and now he says she's in danger.

HRSCNM0612

REQUEST YOUR FREE BOOKS!
2 FREE NOVELS PLUS 2 FREE GIFTS!

✦ Harlequin

ROMANTIC
SUSPENSE

Sparked by Danger, Fueled by Passion.

YES! Please send me 2 FREE Harlequin® Romantic Suspense novels and my 2 FREE gifts (gifts are worth about $10). After receiving them, if I don't wish to receive any more books, I can return the shipping statement marked "cancel." If I don't cancel, I will receive 4 brand-new novels every month and be billed just $4.49 per book in the U.S. or $5.24 per book in Canada. That's a saving of at least 14% off the cover price! It's quite a bargain! Shipping and handling is just 50¢ per book in the U.S. and 75¢ per book in Canada.* I understand that accepting the 2 free books and gifts places me under no obligation to buy anything. I can always return a shipment and cancel at any time. Even if I never buy another book, the two free books and gifts are mine to keep forever.

240/340 HDN FEFR

Name	(PLEASE PRINT)	

Address		Apt. #

City	State/Prov.	Zip/Postal Code

Signature (if under 18, a parent or guardian must sign)

Mail to the **Reader Service:**
IN U.S.A.: P.O. Box 1867, Buffalo, NY 14240-1867
IN CANADA: P.O. Box 609, Fort Erie, Ontario L2A 5X3

Not valid for current subscribers to Harlequin Romantic Suspense books.

Want to try two free books from another line?
Call 1-800-873-8635 or visit www.ReaderService.com.

* Terms and prices subject to change without notice. Prices do not include applicable taxes. Sales tax applicable in N.Y. Canadian residents will be charged applicable taxes. Offer not valid in Quebec. This offer is limited to one order per household. All orders subject to credit approval. Credit or debit balances in a customer's account(s) may be offset by any other outstanding balance owed by or to the customer. Please allow 4 to 6 weeks for delivery. Offer available while quantities last.

Your Privacy—The Reader Service is committed to protecting your privacy. Our Privacy Policy is available online at www.ReaderService.com or upon request from the Reader Service.

We make a portion of our mailing list available to reputable third parties that offer products we believe may interest you. If you prefer that we not exchange your name with third parties, or if you wish to clarify or modify your communication preferences, please visit us at www.ReaderService.com/consumerschoice or write to us at Reader Service Preference Service, P.O. Box 9062, Buffalo, NY 14269. Include your complete name and address.

HRS11B

Harlequin Intrigue® *presents a new installment*
in USA TODAY *bestselling author*
Delores Fossen's miniseries
THE LAWMEN OF SILVER CREEK RANCH.

Enjoy a sneak peek at KADE.

Kade saw it then. The clear bassinet on rollers, the kind
they used in the hospital nursery.

He walked closer and looked inside. There was a baby,
and it was likely a girl, since there was a pink blanket snug-
gled around her. There was also a little pink stretchy cap on
her head. She was asleep, but her mouth was puckered as if
sucking a bottle.

"What does the baby have to do with this?" Kade asked.

"Everything. Two days ago someone abandoned her in the
E.R. waiting room," the doctor explained. "The person left
her in an infant carrier next to one of the chairs. We don't
know who did that, because we don't have security cameras."

Kade was finally able to release the breath he'd been
holding. So this was job related. They'd called him in because he was an FBI agent.

But he immediately rethought that.

"An abandoned baby isn't a federal case," Kade clarified,
though Grayson already knew that. Kade reached down and
brushed his index finger over a tiny dark curl that peeked
out from beneath the cap. "You think she was kidnapped or
something?"

When neither the doctor nor Grayson answered, Kade
looked back at them. The anger began to boil through him.
"Did someone hurt her?"

"No," the doctor quickly answered. "There wasn't a
scratch on her. She's perfectly healthy as far as I can tell."

The anger went as quickly as it had come. Kade had handled the worst of cases, but the one thing he couldn't stomach was anyone harming a child.

"I called Grayson as soon as she was found," the doctor went on. "There were no Amber Alerts, no reports of missing newborns. There wasn't a note in her carrier, only a bottle that had no prints, no fibers or anything else to distinguish it."

Kade lifted his hands palms up. "That's a lot of no's. What do you know about her?" Because he was sure this was leading somewhere.

Dr. Mickelson glanced at the baby. "We know she's about three or four days old, which means she was abandoned either the day she was born or shortly after. She's slightly underweight, barely five pounds, but there was no hospital bracelet. We had no other way to identify her, so we ran a DNA test." His explanation stopped cold, and his attention came back to Kade.

So did Grayson's. "Kade, she's yours."

How does Kade react when he finds out the baby is his?

Find out in KADE.
Available this July wherever books are sold.

This summer, celebrate everything Western
with Harlequin® Books!

www.Harlequin.com/Western
